The Sykes-Weizmann Agreement

A drama and a history

J. A. Jensen

To those who served

The Sykes-Weizmann Agreement

Act I

Scene 1

President's Office, Princeton, New Jersey; Spring, 1903. A secretary leads HORACE KALLEN, a college senior with long, black hair, to a chair in front of a large desk. Kallen looks around the impressive office while he waits.

WOODROW WILSON, a tall man in a three-piece suit with short hair and an imperial bearing, enters. With his chin slightly elevated, he stares for a moment at Kallen and then offers his hand. The two men shake hands and sit.

WILSON: Mr. Kallen, did you have any trouble getting here?

KALLEN: No, President Wilson. I had to change trains in New York, which was a bit of an ant bed, I'm afraid. Too many immigrants.

WILSON: You yourself are an immigrant, are you not?

KALLEN: Yes, sir. I was born in Silesia to a rabbi and his wife. They raised me in Boston.

WILSON: You were complaining about the immigrants.

KALLEN: (smiling) An attempt at humor-- I know there are many complaints about too many immigrants in the country. I was making a joke.

WILSON (without smiling): Yes, a joke. You were making a joke.

KALLEN: Let me just say that I appreciate your invitation to Princeton. I was surprised to be invited because...

A pause.

WILSON: You realize that Princeton has no Jewish instructors?

KALLEN: Yes, sir. Not a big crowd at Temple, I suppose, (He smiles.)

WILSON (no smile): You were invited because William James told me that you were one of his best students graduating this year.

KALLEN: I had the opportunity to study under Professor James and learn something about Pragmatism.

WILSON: So, I understand. William James is now considered one of our leading philosophers and--

KALLEN: --and the founder of psychology.

WILSON (disturbed that Kallen interrupted him): At Princeton, we wait until someone is done speaking before we offer our own thoughts.

KALLEN: Sorry, I interrupted. Never got invited to the Porcellian Club, you know. If you had to wait until you got your turn to speak in my family, you would have grown up completely mute.

(Wilson stands up from his desk and turns away from Kallen. He hides an ever so slight smile. He turns back to Kallen.)

WILSON: Princeton has long been a center for the Southern Presbyterian congregation.

KALLEN: Your father was a Presbyterian minister.

WILSON: How did you know that?

KALLEN: I can't say I didn't prepare to meet the President of Princeton University and I like the name change, incidentally. The College of New Jersey was renamed for the town it occupies. Be glad this university was in a town called Princeton rather than a town called Hoboken.

WILSON: Sir!

KALLEN: Sorry. I just meant the name Princeton sounds very formal. It's a great name for a distinguished university.

WILSON: I'll let the faculty know of your approval. I'm interviewing you today to assess your qualifications to teach English to Princeton freshman. You have done very well at Harvard, but I need to tell you that Princeton has different traditions than does Harvard.

KALLEN: Yes, I understand on game weekends... (he catches himself) Yes sir, it does. I'm sure the differences are significant.

WILSON: Harvard was founded by religious people but now the university has opened itself up to all kinds of different people with different ideas.

KALLEN: Jews.

WILSON: Indeed, it has. Being the son of a Presbyterian minister and a proud graduate of this institution, as president I intend to open Princeton up to some of the same kind of influences.

KALLEN: You are going to hire a Jew to teach English.

WILSON: I am and I am going to hire a Catholic here, as well.

KALLEN (under his breath): The tigers will snarl.

WILSON: Excuse me?

KALLEN: I was just saying that part of education, in my view, is to examine new ideas, to learn about people from new places, and all the while being willing to reflect on one's own values.

WILSON: Yes. I think you are right about that. I am interested in introducing some new influences here at Princeton and I want our students to meet and interact with Jews. The Jewish people are becoming very important citizens of this country and it is important that young men of privilege, even young men of privilege at this historic institution, get to know Jews. I have another motivation for hiring you at Princeton.

KALLEN: Yes, sir.

WILSON: Before I became interested in administrative responsibilities, I taught Latin and Greek history. I believe a proper education requires a man to know something about history and politics. Professor James told me that you read and write Hebrew.

KALLEN: My father is a rabbi, so yes, you could say I have some exposure to Hebrew.

WILSON: Harvard required its graduates to learn Hebrew up until the last century. I'm afraid a respect for ancient languages is not what it once was.

KALLEN: Would I teach Hebrew?

WILSON: We will have to see how you like teaching English here. Sometimes, we find that the young men we hire adapt well to our values; sometimes we ask our community to adapt its social norms and traditions to an individual. I might say though that there are certain cultural values we have at Princeton which will remain constant over time.

KALLEN: Of course.

WILSON (rises from his chair): At Princeton, we believe in something called...character. At this institution, we are guided by traditions of truth. I realize that Professor James claims that truth can be established by the intersection of truth and experience. Pragmatism can be thought of as "what works" as opposed to "what's right." Whenever I am confronted by a problem, I stop to consider what our Savior might have done. Jesus was, of course, a Jew and he was a Jew who sought to teach the world to be a better place. So, when I am confronted by a moral question, I ask myself: what is right?

KALLEN: You demonstrate strong character.

WILSON: Character determines fate, young man, and by standing for truth, we teach character.

KALLEN: Yes, sir.

WILSON: Professor James wrote that you had an interest in the Hebraic roots of Pilgrim thought.

KALLEN: I was only surprised to learn that some members of the faculty referenced the Hebraic precedent for the Pilgrims' decision to leave England and strike out into the wilderness.

WILSON: (rising) I believe you will be an interesting and important faculty member here. I am grateful you rode the train so long to visit with me today and I hope you will consider my offer to teach at Princeton.

Scene 2

Horace Kallen walks to court with LOUIS BRANDEIS, a Boston lawyer who is 20 years older than Kallen. Brandeis struggles with two large legal briefcases and Kallen helps him with one of the briefcases during their discussion.

BRANDEIS: Are you going to take the job or not?

KALLEN: Talking to Wilson was like interviewing with one of the apostles.   Seriously, I'm told he attends prayer service every morning, but I wonder who listens to whom.

BRANDEIS: So, the first Jew to be offered a job at Princeton is going to turn it down?

KALLEN: I hate to hear you put it like that.

BRANDEIS: You should think about whether you might study the law.

KALLEN: I've studied the law. Have you heard of Moses?

BRANDEIS: I'm talking about English law, but you can't do better if you are trying to get into law school than be the first Jew to teach at Princeton. That alone might get you elected to political office.

KALLEN: Jews don't get elected to political office.

BRANDEIS: Give it some time. Jews are going to do very well in America.

(Two young men with beards walk by in long black coats and black hats.)

BRANDEIS: Is this Boston or Minsk?

KALLEN: Those fellows need to live somewhere. They are no longer welcome in Russia. More of them arrive here every day.

BRANDEIS: They aren't going to go very far in those outfits. If they want to live like traditional Jews, they are not in the right country. America is a melting pot.

KALLEN: It tolerates immigrant communities. Immigrants can live in their own neighborhoods for as long as they want to. Why shouldn't the country tolerate Jews who want to live as Jews?

BRANDEIS: How far do you think I would have gone if I'd been wearing a beard and a yamulke?

KALLEN: You're still a Jew. You care about Jews. Every American ends up having to decide how close he wants to stay to his immigrant community and how far he wants to move away from it. It's a tricky balance. This country is not going to allow every Jew trying to get away from the Czar to live in Brooklyn-- Brooklyn or Boston.

BRANDEIS: I'm probably one of the most successful Jewish lawyers in the United States but you could be a more successful lawyer.

KALLEN: If I come back up here for graduate school, I think I'll study with Professor James

BRANDEIS: Pragmatism.

KALLEN: It's a philosophy.

BRANDEIS: A philosophy that says what exactly? Do what works? Isn't pragmatism just being expedient?

KALLEN: It's a little more than that, but as you know more than anyone, philosophy is what guides us in life. It's like the air we breathe. You don't think it's important until it isn't there.

BRANDEIS: You would pass up an opportunity to attend Harvard Law School to study philosophy?

KALLEN: Social theory.

BRANDEIS: I can't decide if you are not as ambitious as I was, or if you are more ambitious.

KALLEN: I want to serve the people like you do. Don't they call you the people's lawyer?

BRANDEIS: The people need a lawyer. The big companies have their lawyers. The rich families have their lawyers. Progressives just want the government to step into the role of squeezing more benefits out of the equation for the common man and his family. The common people don't have the institutions of power.

KALLEN: The institutions of power?

BRANDEIS: The clubs. The social networks. The big money has lobbyists. The lobbyists have their social clubs to push the legislation that benefits their patrons. The people don't have that kind of clout, but we'll put it together. We'll get our own lobbyists. We have a great system in America.

KALLEN: You just need the money. Money buys power here.

BRANDEIS: You must have something to rally around. If you represent a steel monopoly, you work the system for the steel companies. If you are working for garment companies, you push their agenda, and then you use your clubs and secret societies to line up the votes in congress to get things done.

KALLEN: Secret societies?

BRANDEIS: Read up on the Masons. You'll see how power is organized through organizations.

KALLEN: The Masons?

BRANDEIS: That's just an example. There are many interest groups. Churches. Clubs. In the South, they have something they call the Klu Klux Klan. KKK. The members ride around in white robes with hoods on horseback.

KALLEN: I wouldn't want to join a group like that, but I think they have a right to have their opinions. Everyone has a right to an opinion in this country.

BRANDEIS: Talk to me before you decide to pass up law school. Law is the most direct path to politics and politics gives you the greatest impact on the workings of the world. You are a bright young man. Don't waste your light.

Scene 3

Horace Kallen visits Oxford University in 1910 while traveling on a Sheldon Fellowship. Kallen sits with a group of Jewish men, all wearing yarmulkes, in an Oxford common room, but an attractive young woman serves them tea. HARRY SACHER and SAMUEL LANDMAN are British Zionists.

SACHER: I'm afraid I'm not current on the theory of Pragmatism that your Professor James espouses but I can say that we think of his work as primarily an American view. The idea that truth must bear some relationship to practical experience doesn't strike us as exactly revolutionary. We are more interested in his ideas on the workings of the brain.

KALLEN: The evolving field of psychology.

SACHER: Yes. He has founded a new field and we are excited to learn about it.

KALLEN: Fascinating work.

SACHER: That world is a long way from your interest in Zionism.

KALLEN: Not as far as you might think.

SACHER: The truth is that Zionism has a limited appeal to British Jews.

KALLEN: As it does to American Jews, but I believe there is a growing sense that there should be a place that is exclusively for Jews, a place where Jews can live and not feel that they are living in someone else's country.

SACHER: American Jews don't want to leave what they have gained in America and start to plow land in Palestine, do they?

KALLEN: No, but I think there is great sympathy for the idea that there should be such a place. Frankly, many American Jews are not anxious to have so many Russian refugees moving into major cities.

SACHER: Presumably they are poor Jews.

KALLEN: It's not just that the immigrants don't have the same standard of living as Jews already established in the United States, it is also that they have different manners and customs. They might be Jews but some of their behaviors appall non-Jewish and Jewish Americans alike.

SACHER: If we can open Palestine to Jewish migration, the pressure on other countries will be reduced.

KALLEN: Yes, it will, to the extent that the Jews wish to leave Europe, as they have been since the assassination of the Czar.

SACHER: If Jews are identified with political instability, they won't be welcome anywhere. No country wants to have its political traditions determined by a new immigrant class. The perception that the Jews are behind revolutionary movements makes a bad situation worse.

(A beautiful young woman carries in a tray of afternoon scones and jam and places it upon the table. Kallen follows her every move as she comes in, delivers the refreshments, and then leaves.)

KALLEN: The philosophy of Pragmatism allows us to think about how Jews will integrate into the culture of the United States. Up to now, the consensus has been that America must be a melting pot-- that people from different European cultures will mix in America and be assimilated into the culture of the whole.

SACHER: With a loss of Jewish identity.

KALLEN: Exactly, but the strong cultural identification of some of the immigrant groups gives them strength. America is comprised of many different subcultures, and because strong subcultures produce strong families and strong families are at the core of any strong society, America will be a stronger society with the preservation of different subcultures. So, because Judaism believes in the same values as the American founders, there is no conflict between the political aims of the American state and the aims of the Jewish people.

SACHER: So being strongly Jewish doesn't mean you are less American.

KALLEN: That's right. I believe that American Jews might want to strongly support Zionism, a return of the Jews to their traditional lands, while continuing to live in America. Up to now, I think Americans consider loyalty to a foreign power or interest to be against loyalty to America itself. We must change that. Theoretically, there should be no problem with dual loyalty if both sides really have the same cultural goals.

(The young woman enters with a tea kettle of hot water and attracts Kallen's interest once again. She walks out.)

SACHER: I think you find Rachel to be more interesting than our thoughts about Zionism.

KALLEN: I'm sorry to be distracted. She is a lovely young woman.

SACHER: There will always be a conflict between the goals of the British Empire and the goals of Zionism.

LANDMAN: There need not be-- that's his point, Harry.

SACHER: But clearly there is a difference between goals.

LANDMAN: The British Empire does not want all the Jews of Russia to settle right here in England and I dare say that the people of the United States will also object to further large migrations. Therefore, both countries have an interest in a traditional Jewish homeland. Zionists in England share a goal of establishing an alternative for the immigrants.

KALLEN: All this discussion about creating a new Jewish society in ancient Palestine is just talk up to now. Herzl stimulated great interest in the idea, but no one is doing anything about it.

SACHER: Surely, we want to think through the implications of what a new Jewish state might mean before we commit ourselves to it. I believe this would be a perfect subject for a young man interested in so-called Pragmatism. What will be the likely outcomes? How can it be done?

KALLEN: Can it be done? Why think about it and all its various ramifications if there is no practical way it can be accomplished?

LANDMAN: Everything can be done-- it's a matter of waiting for the conditions to be right.

SACHER: Which re-asserts the need to make sure that it is something that we wish to do. Jews in England, France, Germany, and the United States are living very well-- they have much more opportunity than Jews have had for the last 18 centuries. Are we sure it makes so much sense to want to go back to doing every job in a developing economy?

KALLEN: There are a lot of hard jobs in agriculture. Would a Jew from Russia prefer to grow oranges in Palestine or run a store in California?

LANDMAN: Let him choose. The question is whether we can get in a position to give him the choice.

SACHER: Say what you want about Jews: they have not been great colonialists. We don't have the traditions of conquering people and subjecting them to our wishes.

LANDMAN: We can look to the British model.

KALLEN: So maybe the answer is to move non-Jews off from the land in Palestine and help them emigrate to surrounding Arab countries? Wouldn't it be more merciful to just move them out?

LANDMAN: Let's not get too far ahead of ourselves, gentlemen. We are not in Palestine. There are some new Jewish farms there, yes, but it will take many years to build up a Jewish majority in a land like Palestine-- history or no history.

SACHER: Palestine is a little bit like this beautiful Rachel you have become so interested in, Horace. She is lovely, and you might think she will make someone a fine wife and companion-- but she is married. She already has a husband of her own.

KALLEN (shrugs): A man should always be aware of his surroundings. I understand your observation that there is little consensus in the Jewish community for this goal-- little consensus on either side of the Atlantic.

LANDMAN: Keep in mind that it was the Austrians who sparked interest in the movement only ten years ago. There is great interest in Zionism in some Jewish circles: the poorer the people, the greater the interest.

SACHER: Does your fellowship allow you to travel throughout Europe?

KALLEN: That was its original aim. The fellowship was endowed to encourage graduate students to travel in Europe.

LANDMAN: It will be well used this year. There are Jews throughout Europe, from London to St. Petersburg, who are all interested in what will happen next in the Zionist movement. We can put you in touch with them.

SACHER: The danger is that someone will decide to quit talking about the movement and really try to make it happen.

KALLEN: Danger?

SACHER: Danger. There is a price for everything, Horace. We can't pay too much.

Scene 4

Governor Woodrow Wilson wears a boater hat as he makes his way through a political reception in the fall of 1912.

BRANDEIS: Governor, I want you to say hello to my guest this evening.

WILSON: I remember this young man.

KALLEN: It's been almost ten years since you hired me at Princeton, Governor.

WILSON: You did a fine job, Horace. I was happy to see you take the opportunity to return to the study of social philosophy with Professor James. Now I understand you are working in the middle west?

KALLEN: I'm at the University of Wisconsin teaching psychology and philosophy.

WILSON: You must miss the Jewish community of your youth. Wisconsin sounds very quiet when compared with all the activity of Boston, but if you are still visiting Louis Brandeis you will remain close to the action. This man understands that government can't just work for big companies anymore.

BRANDEIS: Governor, I think I spoke to you about the problem of so many Jews coming into the United States.

WILSON: The Jews are an important part of our growing country.

BRANDEIS: Resentments are growing in many cities because the Jews who are coming are not motivated to change their traditional customs. Mr. Kallen here is interested in creating a new choice for Jews who are unhappy in Europe.

KALLEN: Some philanthropic Jews in the United States and Europe started buying property in Palestine some years ago. Most of the land is held by Arabs, but some are willing to trade the land for rather reasonable amounts of money.

BRANDEIS: The idea is that some of the Jews leaving Europe now will have a place to live in the ancient homeland of the Jews.

WILSON: Are Jews moving to Palestine?

BRANDEIS: Some are. They are re-establishing farms not tilled by Jews for the last 18 centuries.

WILSON: That's an amazing development. I've followed Zionism since Theodor Herzl's book ten or fifteen years ago, but I must say I haven't followed it closely. Are the Arabs getting along with their new Jewish neighbors?

BRANDEIS: Well, when the land is purchased, that makes for some very rich Arabs. I believe almost 90,000 acres are now under cultivation.

WILSON: It's a miracle, isn't it? The return of the Jews to Palestine must mark a moment of high religious celebration. Excuse me for a moment. (Wilson steps away to speak to another supporter.)

KALLEN: Did you hear the story of Theodore Roosevelt in front of Jacob Schiff's charity event in New York?

BRANDEIS: Not sure I have.

KALLEN: Roosevelt was in front of the crowd and he told the story of how he came to name Oscar Strauss as Secretary of Commerce. You realize that Strauss was the first Jew to serve in any presidential cabinet?

BRANDEIS: I may have known that.

KALLEN: Well, Roosevelt was telling the story of how he called up Jacob Schiff to ask him who the best man in the country would be for Secretary of Commerce-- not the best Jew, but the best person for the job. As he tells this story, the crowd can see Jacob Schiff sitting and watching the president speak. Schiff is nodding his head and smiling as Roosevelt speaks. Roosevelt wants everyone to understand that he was looking for the best man and not picking the man out of petty political considerations.

BRANDEIS: Doesn't sound so bad.

KALLEN: Then Schiff got up. It was his benefit for Roosevelt. Many people realize that he is stone deaf. So, while he has been smiling as Roosevelt speaks, he couldn't hear a single word that was said.

(A stern appearing Woodrow Wilson now turns back into the circle of Brandeis and Kallen. He begins to listen attentively but Brandeis and Kallen are not yet aware he is listening to the story.)

KALLEN: Schiff re-told the same story Roosevelt had told because he couldn't hear what Roosevelt said.

(Brandeis and Kallen laugh.)

BRANDEIS: Great set up.

KALLEN: Then he said to the crowd that Roosevelt called him up to ask who would make the best "Jew" for the job at Commerce.

(Brandeis and Kallen laugh but then realize that Wilson has rejoined their group and is not laughing. They quickly lose their smiles.)

BRANDEIS: Strauss was a good choice for Commerce.

KALLEN: (coughs) I think he served well. Yes.

WILSON: Excuse me, gentlemen. I was just speaking to a man who told me that the rich Jews will likely vote for Roosevelt again this year. They are unlikely to back a Southerner no matter what his other views are.

BRANDEIS: That's simply not the case, Governor. We're going to see to it that the poor Jews will vote for you. The rich Jews own the garment companies but the poor Jews work for them. Roosevelt and Taft might get the shop owners, but we'll get the workers.

WILSON: The rich Jews are the German Jews and the poor Jews are from Russia?

BRANDEIS: As a rule, I think that might be true. That's the reason we might want you to say something about protecting the Jews who are persecuted in other countries. You might even want to say something about supporting the efforts to relocate refugee Jews in Palestine. That might be a very important issue for the Russian Jews.

WILSON (to Kallen): You will have to stay in touch with Mr. Brandeis here, Horace. If we win this November, maybe he'll end up working in Washington. He might find a way for you to help us.

KALLEN: Yes, Governor. You can count on my support in Wisconsin.

WILSON: I'm glad to hear it. This country hasn't elected a Democrat from the South in 40 years.

BRANDEIS: A son of the South with progressive views; a polite and religious man but with an ear for progressive issues: you have a good chance, Governor.

WILSON: God's Will be done.

Scene 5

Horace Kallen visits his parents in his boyhood home in Boston. His mother goes in and out of the kitchen while his father sits in his library.

MOTHER: Of course, you are staying for dinner. Do you think that you come to visit your parents once a year and you don't stay for dinner?

KALLEN: It's not like I haven't been busy, mother.

MOTHER: I carry you here from Poland and you don't have time to eat dinner?

RABBI KALLEN: He's a busy man. You have left your faith, but you shouldn't abandon your parents.

KALLEN: I haven't really left my faith or my parents. Like other children of immigrant families, I choose not to go to temple.

RABBI KALLEN: Three thousand years of wisdom in one book, but you don't have time to read it.

KALLEN: Please-- I'm only in Boston for a few days. I need your counsel.

RABBI KALLEN: My counsel?

KALLEN: Yours and mother's.

RABBI KALLEN: What subject are we to discuss this evening?

KALLEN: You know that I met Woodrow Wilson with my friend Louis Brandeis during the election campaign.

RABBI KALLEN: Yes, I remember. Your friend Brandeis supported Wilson. I don't know how much it cost him but now that Wilson has been elected, I assume that Brandeis will get a big job in the government.

KALLEN: Why do you think it cost him anything?

RABBI KALLEN: That's the way this political system works. Interested parties give money to the candidate who will represent their interests best. If that candidate wins, some rewards are passed out. I don't think it is a mystery. The political system responds to the marketplace-- very directly to the marketplace.

KALLEN: Do you believe that Brandeis contributed to President Wilson's campaign?

RABBI KALLEN: Son, you are a university professor and you wonder how the political system operates? Of course, he donated money. If you donate enough money, you are also positioned to donate advice. Politicians listen to the people who contribute to their campaigns.

KALLEN: I'm sure you are right about that.

RABBI KALLEN: If the contributors want to get more influence, they find ways of transferring money to the politicians after the election.

KALLEN: Is that legal?

RABBI KALLEN: I'm sure they transfer the money through third parties. People get rich in politics. Why are we talking about this?

KALLEN: Well, President Wilson is going to name his cabinet. It is possible that Brandeis will be named to the cabinet and he might be able to get me a job in Washington.

MOTHER: You're not a lawyer. I told you to go to law school. Do they hire philosophers in Washington?

KALLEN: Not everyone must be a lawyer, mother. Brandeis values good ideas above everything else. He values good ideas and loyalty.

RABBI KALLEN: That sounds right. The system works with money and favors. If you take a job with Brandeis, you will owe him loyalty-- should he ever wish your loyalty.

KALLEN: I mention this because I recently read that Brandeis was changing his mind about Zionism.

RABBI KALLEN: A very bad idea, I think.

KALLEN: I know, I know, but with Jews now being driven out of Russia, why shouldn't they be able to go to Palestine.

RABBI KALLEN: People already live in Palestine-- but the whole idea is crazy. Jews are a people who have done very well, generally very well, living in all the countries of the world. We don't lose our young men to war because we have no borders to defend. We can worship in our faith and trade with Jews in other countries and everyone is benefited. Trade flourishes. Jews get rich. They pay their taxes to their own countries and everyone is better off.

KALLEN: Why are the Russians driving their Jews out of Russia?

RABBI KALLEN: Some young Jews have gotten interested in revolution. That could not be worse for the rest of us. These men are not even Jews. They are atheists. They only revolt for their own economic advantage. They know nothing about their faith.

KALLEN: Do you believe Jews assassinated the Czar?

RABBI KALLEN: Some young Jews have been blamed for that. No Jew I ever met wanted to kill anyone. Proper Jews want to worship as Jews and take care of their families. They do not threaten rulers who command armies. What could be more thoughtless?

KALLEN: My only point is that Jews are emigrating from Russia and they can't all come to America.

RABBI KALLEN: If Jews claim Palestine as their own, what prevents other governments from forcing Jews to go to Palestine? We have freedom here. We have laws that protect us. Why should we go back to the desert?

KALLEN: Brandeis has changed his mind on Zionism. He believes that American Jews have great interest in a return to Palestine.

RABBI KALLEN: American Jews have a great interest in other Jews going to Palestine. American Jews will stay here.

KALLEN: Brandeis might be positioned to support Zionism if he gets the right job.

RABBI KALLEN: Louis Brandeis couldn't pass a Bar Mitzvah. What does he know about being a Jew?

KALLEN: He's very much like me, except that he didn't learn Hebrew or go to Temple.

RABBI KALLEN: My point exactly.

KALLEN: His parents were immigrants from Bohemia-- not so far from our own origins.

RABBI KALLEN: You have both graduated from Harvard and will live important lives in the greatest country in the world. Why would you want anything less for Russian Jews?

KALLEN: Haven't I heard you say "next year in Jerusalem" every year of my childhood?

RABBI KALLEN: That is a phrase that builds unity in the congregation. It shows that we are all Jews and that we share a history and we share a commitment to being Jews in the future. It doesn't mean that we can go back to Jerusalem and build a new temple. Do you think Jews still believe in animal sacrifice? Maybe we should line up some bulls for the holidays? That Jerusalem burned down more than 18 centuries ago. Does Brandeis imagine Palestine remains exactly as we left it?

KALLEN: Americans from England have a homeland; Americans from Italy have a homeland; Americans from Ireland have a homeland. Why shouldn't American Jews have a homeland?

RABBI KALLEN: They do. Their homeland was Palestine-- the Palestine of 18 centuries ago. Italian-Americans are not going back to Italy and Jewish Americans are not going back to Palestine. Go. Visit. Buy some property. But don't imagine that faith will part the seas, my son. Those days are over.

KALLEN: If Brandeis was appointed to a position which allowed him to bring the Jews home to Palestine, shouldn't he try?

RABBI KALLEN: How would an American get in such a position? What interest does this country have in a homeland for the Jews? It doesn't make any sense. Read the lessons of history, Horace; but live in the present day. We can't avenge our loss to the Romans. They won that war but, it turns out, Jewish culture has lasted longer than the Caesars.

Scene 6

Horace Kallen visits his friend Harry Hurwitz at a newspaper office in Cambridge, Massachusetts late in 1912.

HURWITZ: For a college society in its 5th year of existence, I'd say we've done very well. The Menorah Society is now on 60 college campuses.

KALLEN: We founded it!

HURWITZ: That's right, but the society really grew out of a recognition that William James gave to Jewish students. His commendation of Jewish cultural contributions gave us the confidence to be proud of being Jews.

KALLEN: A great man, Dr. James, but the mystery is why others are so loath to give Jews the credit we deserve.

HURWITZ: Jews haven't done so poorly. The Jewish culture remains strong in countries all around the world.

KALLEN: Henry, I wonder what you would think of a new Menorah Society.

HURWITZ: Why? The Menorah Society we have is the best college society for Jews in the United States.

KALLEN: But the college Menorah Society can't get anything done.

HURWITZ: It makes young Jewish students proud of their Jewish heritage.

KALLEN: I understand that, but I wonder if we could come up with a new society—a society for graduates which could organize support for Zionism.

HURWITZ: Why do we need Zionism?

KALLEN: The re-birth of the ancient Jewish state is now possible.

HURWITZ: It's possible but is it desirable?

KALLEN: We need an organization to secretly put a plan for Zionism into action.

HURWITZ: Why would we want to do anything secretly?

KALLEN: Because we want to get it accomplished.

HURWITZ: A secret society for Zionism?

KALLEN: What if we created a new state in Palestine? Wouldn't that solve the problem of Jewish migration?

HURWITZ: What soldiers would protect the land? Jews are not soldiers.

KALLEN: Jews have not been soldiers since ancient times, but they could be again.

HURWITZ: We would have to get legal right to the land. Who would buy it?

KALLEN: We raise the money and go buy the land. The Turkish rulers would have to be willing to sell land to us. The point is that it is now possible. Jews have grown in influence. It is possible to re-establish a Jewish commonwealth in Palestine.

HURWITZ: Theodor Herzl's dream.

KALLEN: His dream but our challenge. If our efforts were known, the American public would suspect us of working behind the scenes to advance the cause of a new Israel.

HURWITZ: Which is exactly what we would be doing.

KALLEN: If there could be a new Zion, wouldn't it be worthwhile? Wouldn't the ends justify the means?

HURWITZ: It would be dramatic: a new Jewish state arising in the same ancient land of the old.

KALLEN: Zionism is a great goal and I intend to facilitate it. We will organize a secret society complete with secret oaths and secret communications. It is essential that only the best men and women be involved. We will establish a new Jewish commonwealth, a just state, a state founded on the sanctity of labor and the equality of the classes. The Jews will lead the world into a new era of governance.

HURWITZ: You propose a secret society with secret methods.

KALLEN: That's right. We only recruit the most devoted Zionists-- people who are willing to sacrifice everything for the cause of the re-establishment of a Jewish state.

(The lights dim as the men on the stage change positions and the light rises on Kallen as he gives the oath of the Parushim to his friend Henry Hurwitz.)

KALLEN: "You are about to take a step which will bind you to a single cause for all your life. You will for one year be subject to an absolute duty whose call you will be impelled to heed at any time, in any place, and at any cost. And ever after, until our purpose shall be accomplished, you will be a fellow of a brotherhood whose bond you will regard as greater than any other in your life-- dearer than that of family, of school, of nation."

"By entering this brotherhood, you become a self-dedicated soldier in the army of Zion. Your obligation to Zion becomes your paramount obligation... It is the wish of your heart and of your own free will to join our fellowship, to share its duties, its tasks, and its necessary sacrifices."

HURWITZ (the light shifts from Kallen to Hurwitz): "Before this council, in the name of all that I hold dear and holy, I hereby vow myself, my life, my fortune, and my honor to the restoration of the Jewish nation, to its restoration as a free and autonomous state, by its laws perfect in justice, by its life enriching and preserving the historic speech, the culture, and the ideals of the Jewish people."

"To this end I dedicate myself in behalf of the Jews, my people, and in behalf of all mankind."

"To this end I enroll myself in the fellowship of the Parushim. I pledge myself utterly to guard and to obey and to keep secret the laws and the labor of the fellowship, its existence and its aims. Amen"

Scene 7

Louis Brandeis boards an overnight ferry boat from South Yarmouth to New York City with Horace Kallen and FELIX FRANKFURTER in late August 1914. They stand on an outside deck and watch the lights on the mainland disappear in the distance.

BRANDEIS: I always like to watch the lights on the shore grow dim. Nice night to be out here.

KALLEN: Nice to be out here with no guns shooting at us. The guns are now blazing in Europe.

FRANKFURTER: They are all cousins-- that's what is so remarkable. The ruling monarchs of Russia and Europe are all related. What a bunch of fools!

BRANDEIS: They should have had some better way to avoid mobilization. Insane to turn army against army.

FRANKFURTER: Horrible loss of life.

KALLEN: What do our friends say about Russia? Will the Jews in Russia be compelled to fight for the Czar?

FRANKFURTER: If Jews live in Russia, they will fight for the Czar. If they live in Germany, they will fight for the Kaiser. Ridiculous.

KALLEN: I suppose that is the logical end of assimilation. Russian Jews are Russian; German Jews are Germans.

BRANDEIS: But they are still Jews. They shouldn't be fighting each other.

FRANKFURTER: You will now lead the biggest organization for Jews in the United States. You are positioned well to look out for the Jews during the war.

BRANDEIS: I still can't believe that Jacob Schiff told Wilson I wasn't a real Jew-- that crazy old bastard.

FRANKFURTER: Would we be better off if you were in the cabinet?

BRANDEIS: I should have been Attorney General.

FRANKFURTER: That would have prevented your service to Zionism. You weren't asked to be in the cabinet, but you were then able to become the most prominent Jew in America by promoting the Zionist cause.

BRANDEIS: If I'd been Attorney General, I couldn't have taken the job with the Zionists.

FRANKFURTER: Who is to say that your influence with President Wilson is not greater now than it would have been?

BRANDEIS: It probably is greater with me out of Washington. He's taken every suggestion I've made.

KALLEN: You have built your influence by supplying Wilson with good ideas.

BRANDEIS: I've built my influence the same way everyone builds influence in the political world: contributions were made; appointments were arranged; friends were accumulated. It helps if you are on the right side. I was once a lawyer for the big companies; then I realized that greater good lay with working for the people.

FRANKFURTER: It sounds better: the people's lawyer.

BRANDEIS: Favorable publicity never hurts. Let's just say that I have built a relationship with President Wilson where he comes to me.

KALLEN: That's influence.

BRANDEIS: Yes, and I'm going to persuade Jacob Schiff to fund the causes we represent. He's going to fund a professorship for you at the law school and he's going to fund our efforts in Palestine. Schiff will contribute as much as we ask.

FRANKFURTER: Maybe Schiff did you a favor to push you toward Zionism.

BRANDEIS: Maybe, but we will have to see how this war plays out. The Ottoman Empire has ruled over the Middle East for 400 years. Maybe Jewish interests will have a place at the peace conference.

KALLEN: Why would Jews send a delegation to a peace conference? If Jews live in other countries, wouldn't they be represented by those countries?

BRANDEIS: Let's see what kind of friends we make during the war. If the Germans win, maybe our German friends can influence the Ottomans to give us Palestine. If the French, Russians, and English win, perhaps we can urge those governments to try to solve the problem of Jewish migration at the peace conference.

KALLEN: I still say that secrecy is critical in our undertakings. It is critical to the work of my secret society of Zionists and it is even more critical to any efforts you might make with President Wilson.

BRANDEIS: Our efforts must remain secret. I agree with that, but there is also too much we don't know. We don't know how long this war will last or what the world will look like when it is over.

KALLEN: We don't know what opportunities will arise, but we do know that we represent the interests of Zionist Jews in the United States. We know that wars rarely turn out as predicted.

FRANKFURTER: We are sailing into the night: we know where we want to land but we can't see our course ahead.

Act II

Scene 1

Harry Sacher and Samuel Landman walk outside a synagogue in London in the spring of 1915.

SACHER: When Turkey entered the war, I think every Jew who has ever entertained a Zionist thought was jolted into the realization that it could finally happen.

LANDMAN: That the Zionist dream could be realized?

SACHER: Yes, for the first time in 400 years, Palestine might be freed from the Ottomans. With the Turks in the war and the British in the war, if the British win, the Turks might be compelled to give up Palestine. It could be one of the terms of surrender.

LANDMAN: Are you a Zionist?

SACHER: Certainly not, but we're all Jews. You and I are Jews who live in England. I think Lucien Wolf feels the same way. Jews have been accepted in England for more than two generations. We live our lives as Catholics live their lives. The days of religious persecution are over in England.

LANDMAN: The Russian Jews hope for a return to the Promised Land.

SACHER: What the Russian Jews don't understand is that the Promised Land of the Bible has been occupied for the last 18 centuries by Arabs.

LANDMAN: A few Jews in Jerusalem.

SACHER: Yes. Amazingly, some Jews continued to live in Jerusalem, but the reality is that Jews left Palestine in Roman times and became the first international people. There are Jews in every country-- almost every country-- and now the Russian Jews believe that Jews should own Palestine so that Jewish farms can be re-established.

LANDMAN: Isn't that the great Jewish dream?

SACHER: As a cultural goal, yes, but as a practical reality, no. The Jews were a racially distinct group then; now, they have mixed with peoples throughout the world. Do you realize that there are Jews living in Africa who are black and Jews from Asia who actually appear oriental? They don't look like English Jews.

LANDMAN: Jews are not a distinct race.

SACHER: You and I recognize that Jews are not a race, but the Russian Jews believe we are. Russian Jews look like other Russian Jews and most of them have never seen African Jews.

LANDMAN: Do they think we are still one tribe?

SACHER: Some people who call for a return to Palestine believe that we are one race, one people. You and I understand that it has taken many generations for Jews to be accepted here in England and we have been accepted in England because of the reality that Jews do not have a physical country. There is no homeland for Jews. Now, the Russian Jews argue that we should have a physical country. I say, when there is a Jewish homeland, why should the English continue to allow our residence and prosperity in England?

LANDMAN: We were born in England.

SACHER: Of course, we were. You don't have to convince me, but the English worker doesn't understand why Jews should compete for jobs with him. If there is a Jewish homeland, when times get tough, he will want the Jews to go home.

LANDMAN: Save your thoughts. Do you see who approaches? I believe that is Chaim Weizmann.

CHAIM WEIZMANN enters with a briefcase and an umbrella.

WEIZMANN: Good afternoon, friends. I never carried an umbrella in Russia or Germany.

SACHER: Good afternoon, Dr. Weizmann. Have you had time to study the workings of the government?

WEIZMANN: Who would have ever thought a Jew could gain acclaim in the British Empire by studying biochemistry?

SACHER: We've heard that you are trying to sell Zionism to government figures and the most elite Jews.

WEIZMANN: I've met some very important people here, including some very wealthy people by the name of Rothschild.

LANDMAN: Then the rumors are true.

WEIZMANN: The Rothschilds can introduce me to Herbert Samuel.

SACHER: His cousin is Lord Montagu.

WEIZMANN: I didn't know they were related.

SACHER: Lord Montagu was once Montagu Samuel-- he reversed his names to Samuel Montagu. Edwin Samuel Montagu.

WEIZMANN: He changed his name, but he can't change his nationality, can he?

LANDMAN: He doesn't want to. Montagu is a very observant Jew. He's visited Palestine many times and has purchased property there.

WEIZMANN: Then he is a Zionist after all.

SACHER: We're all Zionists on some level; we just see it differently.

WEIZMANN: Are you now thinking that it might be a possibility?

SACHER: I can see a state where Jews who wish to buy property from their Arab neighbors, could live as Jews. That would allow those who want to live in Palestine to live in Palestine. I think many Englishman would be happy to see them go.

WEIZMANN: That's what we are trying to accomplish.

SACHER: That's not what I've been told. You are trying to create a state only for Jews. My question has always been: what will happen to the Arabs who have lived there for the last 18 centuries?

WEIZMANN: It is land promised to the Jews.

SACHER: We can't create a state where we would discriminate based on religion. How can we ask the English not to discriminate based on religion and then we create a state where Jews would claim special rights based on their religion? That makes no sense.

WEIZMANN: Many things in our history make no sense, but the time has arrived to reclaim the land God promised to us.

SACHER: God promised? You believe you can claim a divine right to land? Do the English have a divine right to England? Do the Germans have a blood right to Germany?

WEIZMANN: Our disagreements are trivial.

LANDMAN: I received a letter from an American professor this week. You should know about his interest in Zionism.

WEIZMANN: An American professor?

LANDMAN: A man whom Harry and I met when he was touring Europe on an academic fellowship a few years ago. He was interested in Zionism. I believe he got a doctoral degree with the American philosopher William James.

WEIZMANN: The American philosopher who is writing brilliant things about the workings of the brain.

LANDMAN: That's the man.

WEIZMANN: What is this young Zionist's name?

LANDMAN: Horace Kallen. Now, he is at the University of Wisconsin now, but he was with James in Massachusetts.

WEIZMANN: What did he write to you?

LANDMAN: Kallen believes that the English should be willing to deliver Palestine to the Jews-- if the Jews side with England and the Allies in the war.

WEIZMANN: Surely, he can't believe the idea originated with him?

LANDMAN: He is not claiming originality.

SACHER: Every Zionist I know claims the same idea.

LANDMAN: He writes that he has organized a secret society.

WEIZMANN: What does his secret society do?

LANDMAN: The society is called the "Parushim" and it recruits Jews to work secretly to establish a Jewish commonwealth in Palestine.

WEIZMANN: I should know this man.

LANDMAN: You should, indeed.

WEIZMANN: What does a secret society add to our efforts?

LANDMAN: He believes he can deliver what everyone else is just talking about.

WEIZMANN: What is that?

LANDMAN: He thinks that if the English were to issue a public statement in favor of giving the Jews Palestine, American Jews would throw their considerable political influence behind American entry into the war.

WEIZMANN: What political influence does he think American Jews have?

SACHER: He might have a point there, Dr. Weizmann. American Jews have done very well.

WEIZMANN: They are what? Maybe two million? They are two million in a country of 100 million. That's not many votes.

SACHER: We know the Jews have great influence. Jews own many important newspapers-- newspapers which forge public opinion.

WEIZMANN: I wonder how many newspapers he is talking about.

SACHER: Besides newspapers, they have many businesses which command political power, sometimes through contributions.

WEIZMANN: I'm not in the business of discouraging people who share my goal of restoring the Jewish nation.

SACHER: Remember that it was probably never purely Jewish. The Bible records many other peoples.

WEIZMANN: The details can be resolved.

LANDMAN: I was thinking that if we could get his letter to Herbert Samuel, Samuel could get it considered by the cabinet.

WEIZMANN: Why don't you show me the letter? I'd like to read it before too many others. Professor Horace Kallen might need to teach us something about secrecy. We need to get our goal accomplished and secrecy might be a necessary condition.

SACHER: Isn't that the basis of Pragmatism? Isn't the philosophy of Pragmatism to do what works? Do what gets results?

WEIZMANN: I haven't studied Pragmatism, but I'd like to see Professor Kallen's proposal. It's hard to believe he can do something we can't do.

LANDMAN: He can't do anything without our help. If we don't get the British to agree to deliver Palestine, there is no deal; but if we could, maybe Mr. Kallen could provide some important political power for us in the United States.

Scene 2

LORD HERBERT KITCHENER walks with SIR MARK SYKES into a meeting with Prime Minister H. H. ASQUITH, DAVID LLOYD GEORGE, and Foreign Secretary SIR EDWARD GREY in Whitehall in January 1916.

KITCHENER: Sir Mark has returned from Cairo with a current assessment of the prospects for an Arab revolt. I wanted everyone to hear his report.

ASQUITH: I would have thought you might want to spend more time at Sledmere. Have you really been in Egypt?

SYKES: Sledmere will still be home when the war is over, Prime Minister. We're all doing our duty.

ASQUITH: Indeed, you are.

SYKES: Lord Kitchener proposed an Arab revolt to Grand Sharif Hussein fourteen months ago and it now appears that the Sharif has concluded that Arab independence would be an excellent outcome of the present conflict.

GREY: An independent Arab kingdom with himself as the ruler, I assume.

SYKES: Right. The Grand Sharif has four sons who also figure into the equation. At present, they have established contact with other Arab nationalists under Ottoman control. Obviously, the Ottomans would like the Grand Sharif to endorse the jihad that they have proclaimed against the British infidels, but the Ottomans have not promised Arab independence or support for the Grand Sharif after the war.

GREY: Can the Arabs really mount a revolt against the Turks? Do they have an army?

SYKES: They have great spirit and courage but at present they lack guns and an army.

LLOYD GEORGE: Surely, you can't think the Grand Sharif will be able to carry out a meaningful attack on the Turks.

SYKES: The Grand Sharif might not command an army, but his support for us, or lack of support for the Turks, could tip the scales in this theater.

LLOYD GEORGE: One division of Turks with machine guns would be able to destroy all those fellows riding with drawn swords on horseback.

KITCHENER: The Arabs have no army, but they have the advantage of being the occupants of the entire Middle East. So, to have them revolt against the Turks prevents the Turks from turning them against our position in Egypt. If we could arm them, we would have a strong ally against Turkey.

SYKES: If the Arabs join with the Turks and support their rulers, our position in the entire area will be threatened-- including Cairo, including the Suez Canal. India might be lost.

ASQUITH: Is our intent to rule these nations after the war?

KITCHENER: Churchill says that we shouldn't leave the area under the rule of the Turks and I agree. We will be able to advise them with respect to governmental institutions and organization of their security while protecting our interests.

ASQUITH: We must answer a fundamental question: is the British Empire stronger with more land and people to rule or are we already overstretched?

KITCHENER: We don't want to conquer that part of the world and then relinquish it to competing powers after the war.

ASQUITH: Yet Lord Haldane continues to point out that permanent peace cannot be obtained without consensus. If we take German land or re-arrange the borders of these ancient religious lands, we will face further wars ten or twenty years hence. The Home Secretary Reginald McKenna agrees that we should suggest that no power should take anything from this war. To do so would be destabilizing for the community of nations after this madness has been stopped.

GREY: As stop it certainly must.

SYKES: The Arabs ask for money and for guns.

KITCHENER: We can supply them if they perform on their revolt. If the revolt does not materialize, no further guns or money will arrive.

ASQUITH: We have received a proposal from an American professor in Wisconsin who believes that we should issue a public statement in favor of giving the Jews Palestine after the war. He believes it will win the loyalty of American Jewry-- who could lobby for American intervention.

GREY: The Americans continue to proclaim their neutrality.

ASQUITH: Exactly. President Wilson shows no signs of changing his mind. If anything, Mr. Wilson proposes the end of imperial rule.

KITCHENER: We do not have control of Palestine. How can we give the Jews land we do not possess?

LLOYD GEORGE: We could mount an offensive from Egypt and invade Palestine.

KITCHENER: What is your experience with commanding armies, Mr. Lloyd George? Have you ever visited Egypt?

LLOYD GEORGE: My work has kept me mostly here in England.

KITCHENER: Yes, and you represented the Zionist interests in the Uganda proposal a decade ago.

LLOYD GEORGE: I'm aware of their desire for Palestine, yes, but I have no love of the Jews.

KITCHENER: Unless it is an election year and then I'm sure you find their support to be most important.

LLOYD GEORGE: The Jews contribute to many campaigns.

KITCHENER: I'm sure they do and I'm sure they contribute to elections in the United States, as well.

LLOYD GEORGE: That's the system we have, Lord Kitchener. Same rules for all.

KITCHENER: One of our own members of the cabinet, Herbert Samuel, has proposed that it be the goal of the British army to secure Palestine for the Jews. The question we need to answer here is whether we are spilling British blood to fight for the British Empire or to fight for a future Jewish empire?

LLOYD GEORGE: Having Jews in Palestine could improve our defense of the Suez Canal and buffer our position in Egypt.

KITCHENER: Could it? Having spent a good part of my military career in Egypt and having published a survey of Syria and Palestine, I can say with some military and geographical experience that capturing Palestine would serve exactly no strategic interest of ours in the Middle East. Lord Montagu, Herbert Samuel's cousin, came to the same conclusion. Montagu has been outspoken on the point. He is a British Jew who is thinking about what is best for the British Empire.

ASQUITH: To what extent should we support the Arab revolt?

KITCHENER: That at least makes some sense: the Arabs live in the area. To make a public proclamation that we support Zionist goals in Palestine would fully antagonize the Grand Sharif. He would endorse the jihad and perhaps lead an attack to free Egypt of British rule. The Islamic faith is dominant throughout the region. Why would we seek to support the Jews in Palestine? There are few Jews in Palestine. What army do the Jews bring to the conflict? The army of the press? Publicity? Or the army of the purse?

GREY: Will the Arabs bring much to the battle?

KITCHENER: If we supply them with guns and money, they will not work against us. They will interrupt communication, cut railroad routes, generally cause trouble. If the Arab revolt only makes the Arab an enemy of the Turk, we will have won a great battle.

Scene 3

Louis Brandeis sits at his desk at the Zionist offices in New York and opens an envelope which contains a letter and a few dollars of American currency. Horace Kallen enters the office.

BRANDEIS: My God, my God. There has never been anything like this.

KALLEN: It's better than a political campaign.

BRANDEIS: It's very much like a political campaign, I would guess. You have come up with an issue that drives these old rich Jews to open their purses and give.

KALLEN: They are responding to your speeches. When you say that "to be better Americans, Jews must be better Jews; and to be better Jews, they must give to Zionism," the audiences are won over.

BRANDEIS: That was your argument. You were the one who convinced me that Jews can live in America and be proud of practicing their religion. Our cultural strength makes our nation stronger. That was a brilliant insight.

KALLEN: It was the insight of William James.

BRANDEIS: You translated his work into a new way of looking at America. It's not a melting pot; it's a sculpture garden. These Jews are voting with their dollars. They love the idea of a new Jewish commonwealth in Palestine.

KALLEN: We have our enemies. I had to get Hurwitz to write a column for a newspaper in Cleveland. One of the rabbis out there has started a campaign against us.

BRANDEIS: He'll have to change his opinions if he wants to keep his congregation. Zionism is selling better than that new bottled soda water.

KALLEN: The rabbi's objections are heart felt: he believes that if Jews move to Palestine, they will antagonize the Arabs who live there now.

BRANDEIS: It doesn't have to be like that.

KALLEN: Not if it is properly designed. If we can design the new Palestine to protect the rights of women and people of other faiths, we will have created a model for all other nations to follow.

BRANDEIS: A place where labor is honored, and the society is not ruled by the rich.

KALLEN: That is our dream, but we can't achieve it unless Zionism prevails. Zionism will not prevail if we have rabbis attacking us in the newspapers.

BRANDEIS: Do you have Hurwitz attacking right back?

KALLEN: We have members of the Parushim writing columns all over the country: we have members who are editors; we have members who are writers; and we have prosperous and influential Jews agitating for our goals. We are here to push public opinion.

BRANDEIS: We are here to push public opinion in the direction of Zionism and we must put some of these dollars back into circulation. How much are you paying Hurwitz?

KALLEN: Very little. He's getting paid as a journalist.

BRANDEIS: Well, let's put this money to the work the donors have requested. We are not able to buy land yet, but we are able to keep our machine well-oiled and maintained. I want Hurwitz to get $100 and give Walter Lippmann $100. He works with us.

KALLEN: That's more money than an American soldier makes in six months.

BRANDEIS: Good. If they are working for our goals, they are working for us. $100. I want you to give the candidates for congress each $100.

KALLEN: The Democrats?

BRANDEIS: Yes, the Democrats, and give the Republicans $100, as well.

KALLEN: Aren't there laws restricting how much money we can give?

BRANDEIS: Are there laws which restrict campaign contributions? Let me think about that question for a minute. That would mean that a majority of the politicians would have to write a law, and then pass it, and then get the president to sign it, which would protect the public from interested parties.

KALLEN: Are there such laws?

BRANDEIS: In a word? No. There are no such laws. You can give politicians as much money as they will take, and believe me they will take as much as you'll give them.

KALLEN: Isn't that like a bribe?

BRANDEIS: It is exactly like a bribe, like a legal bribe, and it is done throughout this great country of ours. There are no laws restricting how much money we can give each other nor for what purpose.

KALLEN: Surely, bribery is illegal.

BRANDEIS: If it can be shown to be bribery for a specific purpose. It all comes down to how the money is given. Giving money to Hurwitz is not illegal, believe me.

KALLEN: What if we give a rabbi some money for his temple.

BRANDEIS: Not illegal.

KALLEN: Are politicians required to report the money?

BRANDEIS: No, and they don't; so, don't worry about it.

KALLEN: That would mean that rich people could get almost anything they want.

BRANDEIS: That's what it means. Do you know Henry Morgenthau?

KALLEN: The Ambassador to Turkey?

BRANDEIS: Yes, the Ambassador to Turkey. He was President Wilson's campaign treasurer. He's a smart Jew who bought up real estate next to subway stops in New York.

KALLEN: Was he buying the land with inside information?

BRANDEIS: Let's just say he bought the land. We don't know what information he had, and he isn't going to tell us. He made a fortune and he gave some to a man named Woodrow Wilson when Wilson needed it. Now, he is the Ambassador to Turkey.

KALLEN: I think he's been a good ambassador.

BRANDEIS: Excellent. My point is only that the capitalistic system works by deploying capital. It isn't a secret. We are running an enterprise now to promote the dream of Zionism. You came up with the philosophical justification for why Jews don't have to worry about so-called "dual loyalty," and I give speeches promoting a goal that only 3 years ago, I opposed. Zionism has a life of its own. We are working for that vision now. We are going to take this money and money that we raise around the country and we are going to pay our friends who support our cause and pay our friends who heckle our critics. You have expenses. You will need to have some of those expenses covered.

KALLEN: I couldn't take money from the Zionist cause.

BRANDEIS: You are the Zionist cause. There is no better investment Zionism could make than invest in you. Furthermore, you will use this money to contribute to the political careers of people who support Zionism.

KALLEN: Here in New York?

BRANDEIS: Yes, here in New York, and you will invest money in New Jersey and in Connecticut. Those states have representatives. You must make sure they understand where the money is coming from. Politicians must understand that they owe you a favor. Make sure you keep the cancelled checks

KALLEN: Why keep the checks?

BRANDEIS: To have some leverage on the politicians if they can't remember who put them in office. They have a way of forgetting their friends when you need something from them.

KALLEN: That doesn't seem right.

BRANDEIS: No, it doesn't seem right but that's the best way ever devised. Let me tell you something else: I want you to give some money to our friends in England and in France.

KALLEN: That can't be legal.

BRANDEIS: Why don't you let me worry about our legal position. You go meet with the politicians I tell you to and give them the money I tell you to give. Maybe you don't have to go to Russia, but there are some Jews in Russia who need to share our vision. If we get enough money, we will give it to whomever we think will best advance the cause of Zionism.

KALLEN: That's our responsibility?

BRANDEIS: That's our responsibility. The people who are putting their hard-earned dollars into these envelopes and writing their heartfelt letters for Zionism deserve to have us advance their cause. That's what we're going to do: we're going to invest this money into the dream of a new Jewish commonwealth in Palestine.

KALLEN: The crowds only seem to get bigger. You are striking a nerve with these people and you never endured a Bar Mitzvah. You don't even speak Hebrew.

BRANDEIS: There are plenty of those orthodox Jews out there. I'm like a politician. I'm the most attractive candidate for Zionist sentiment right now. We take our message around the country and we rally support for a Jewish homeland, and then we invest the money quietly, secretly, with people who can help us achieve our goal.

KALLEN: How do we know these people will work for Zionism?

BRANDEIS. It's an election year. Sit down and start writing checks. I'll show you how to make some friends in the world of politics.

Scene 4

Sir Mark Sykes stands in front of a map of the Middle East in the Foreign Office in early 1916 with Francois Georges-Picot, the first secretary of the French embassy, with a crayon in his hand. Sykes colors in Mesopotamia with a red crayon.

SYKES: If the Russians take Constantinople, as they say they will, that leaves us to divide what remains of the Ottoman Empire.

PICOT: With an ordinary crayon?

SYKES: Monsieur Picot: We are standing at the center of the Foreign Office of the greatest empire to rule the world since the Romans.

PICOT: When it is combined with the French Empire.

SYKES: Yes, of course. I did not forget the prominence of the French Empire. Under the direction of two countries, which you and I so humbly represent today, much of the world's population currently labors. (He turns and smiles at Picot.) Crayons are within our rather modest budget.

PICOT: Both countries were early to develop laws and governments and begin to trade with distant lands.

SYKES: Which led us to assist people without proper laws and governments to establish their own. France has done much to improve the societies of the eastern Mediterranean and I'm sure your government will want to continue that influence.

PICOT: France will take the eastern Mediterranean and have an area of influence over the Arab Empire in Syria. (He colors the region with a blue crayon.)

SYKES: The Russians agree that the sites holy to the world's great religions will remain under international control. (Sykes colors the Holy sites with a brown crayon.)

PICOT: A condominium of powers.

SYKES: Right. An international condominium of powers. The Arabs would like to control the entire region themselves.

PICOT: I'm sure they would, but there are French business interests in these areas which will need protection and supervision. We did not invest the capital to develop these lands completely as an act of charity. Development costs francs and we intend to protect our investments.

SYKES: Rightly so. These countries have been under Ottoman rule for the last 400 years. The Ottomans have not agreed to withdraw their jurisdiction over the Arabs after the war, so the Arabs have little reason to wish to stay loyal to the Ottomans.

PICOT: If the Arabs could overthrow the Ottomans, they would. They have no guns. They have no armies. The Ottomans would crush any revolt and be merciless with the revolutionaries.

SYKES: I was meeting with a representative of the Grand Sharif just a month ago and one of our fellows cranked up the wireless to send a message to Cairo.

PICOT: Using the radio?

SYKES: Yes, he was just generating some power to run the wireless unit and was able to establish contact with Cairo. The Arab man had never seen such technology before-- he was overwhelmed. Shocked. He passed his hand above and below the wireless unit to be sure that we were not trying to trick him.

The two men laugh.

PICOT: We should remember that the first Russian offensive of this war was performed on horseback. Imagine. Even the Czar's generals were overwhelmed to witness the destructive power of the machine gun.

SYKES: The poor Arabs are sporting long and beautiful swords; and I'm sure they would use beautiful horses in the attack, but times have changed, and they will be no match for the Turks.

PICOT: Yet they wish to rule themselves.

SYKES: A good ambition, I believe, at the proper time.

PICOT: I hear rumors that the American president favors peoples of the countries of the world choosing their own governments.

SYKES: Surely, he means the people of the countries of Europe.

PICOT: No, he means the people of the countries of the world. He has made it clear: he calls for the end of colonialism.

SYKES: If he favors self-government in the Middle East after this war, I'm afraid he will meet resistance. Imperialistic empires are haunted by problems, by abuses, but they offer the best way forward. The thought of the peoples of the subcontinent governing themselves is quite frankly absurd. If Britain leaves, chaos will take her place.

PICOT: We may have our differences of opinion, but this plan will satisfy your government and mine and the Russians if the Holy Land is ruled by all governments. We agree that Palestine belongs to all.

SYKES: Yes, I think we can look back at the crusades through the centuries and conclude that enough blood has been spilt over Palestine.

Scene 5

Lord Kitchener, dressed as a Field Marshal rather than as Secretary of State for War, strides into the 10 Downing Street office of the Prime Minister.

ASQUITH: You have served too long to be rattled by some bad press.

KITCHENER: I've weathered attacks before. I had my critics in the Boer War when discipline was meted out.

ASQUITH: Then you proceeded to India where you served with great distinction.

KITCHENER: In Egypt, we had enough trouble with the enemy-- we didn't have to worry about the press. We had problems with supplies there, too.

ASQUITH: Resigning your command is out of the question. I cannot run this government without a man of your experience and distinction. These are minor skirmishes with the press.

KITCHENER: We all know that I was the first to argue that the war would last much longer than anticipated. I was the one who pressed for the orders for extra weapons. The fact that the rifles have not been delivered does not negate the fact that I was the one who ordered them. I can't go to the United States and make the rifles myself.

ASQUITH: No. No one says otherwise.

KITCHENER: Yet, I must endure these attacks from our own press saying that I have not administered the war efficiently. Imagine these journalists presuming to know anything about the conduct of a war. If this were South Africa, I'd have that reporter taken out and flogged.

ASQUITH: No, you wouldn't.

KITCHENER: Yes, I would, and I'd put the publisher in jail. Do you think the Germans allow their war effort to be criticized in their press?

ASQUITH: We are an open society and enduring criticism is part of the job.

KITCHENER: Have you read Leo Maxse's National Review?

ASQUITH: I know about his paper, but I don't read it regularly.

KITCHENER: He criticizes some of our newspapers for being controlled by German Jews. Of course, they find fault in my administration of the war--they want me to capture Palestine for the Jews. It is not more complicated than that.

ASQUITH: The Jews carry some influence with the press but so does everyone else. The rifles will soon be delivered, and this crisis will have passed.

KITCHENER: Then they will find something else to criticize. They will say that I put too few divisions in France and then change attack and claim that I've put in too many-- I don't have enough divisions here to protect against a German invasion. We are pressed here to cover our defense of the home island and I don't favor an invasion of Palestine. Just the suggestion of supporting Zionism might push the Arabs back into the arms of the Turks.

ASQUITH: It is hard for me to understand why Herbert Samuel presses for Palestine. It's like Disraeli said: "race is everything."

KITCHENER: Disraeli was working for England. If you are a Jew serving in the British cabinet, you should be thinking about the welfare of Britain, not the welfare of the Jews in Russia or Poland or Germany. Look at a map: what do we gain by occupying Palestine?

ASQUITH: With Winston's folly at Gallipoli, I hope they see that we can't afford to dilute our strength. This war is a stalemate and should end.

KITCHENER: Lloyd George believes we should invade Palestine to capture the Holy Land. When did he become such a missionary? He wants to capture Palestine because he is being well paid to take that position and now he is in charge of munitions-- he'll be able to reward those who sponsor him.

ASQUITH: Lloyd George speaks according to his mood and his company. Give him a different audience and he'll give you a different opinion.

KITCHENER: He claims to be a religious man, but it seems he has a problem with fornication. Your chief military adviser is a retired field marshal who has commanded troops in every major British battle for the last 30 years. Lloyd George has no military experience and his chief military adviser is a Russian immigrant by the name of Weizmann. How does he have the nerve to criticize our war efforts?

ASQUITH: We will not invade Palestine while you and I control the war; and we should stop this madness as soon as the Germans are willing. We are accomplishing exactly nothing.

KITCHENER: The Germans possess a great advantage with their U boats. Their submarines are more effective than our mines.

ASQUITH: Haldane is right: we should propose a truce wherein nothing is taken by anyone. We should keep the borders where they are and, in that way, insure the peace for another century.

KITCHENER: I'm off to Russia next week if the revolutionaries don't topple the government before I arrive. It's time to put down the revolutionaries in Russia; and it is time to demand loyalty right here. The press should be working with us, not against us.

Scene 6

HERBERT SAMUEL, the cousin of British anti-Zionist Lord Montagu but a Zionist member of the British Cabinet, reads from his January 1915 "secret" Memorandum to the Cabinet, <u>The Future of Palestine</u>, now declassified.

SAMUEL: "The course of events opens a prospect of a change, at the end of the war, in the status of Palestine. Already there is a stirring among the twelve million Jews scattered throughout the countries of the world. A feeling is spreading with great rapidity that now...some advance may be made...towards the fulfillment of the hope and desire, held with unshakable tenacity for eighteen hundred years, for the restoration of the Jews to the land to which they are attached.

If the attempt were made to place the 400,000 or 500,000 Mohammedans of Arab race under a Government which rested upon the support of 90,000 or 100,000 Jewish inhabitants, there can be no assurance that such a Government, even if established by authority of the Powers, would be able to command obedience....

I am assured that the solution of the problem of Palestine which would be much the most welcome to the leaders and supporters of the Zionist movement throughout the world would be the annexation of the country to the British Empire...It would, no doubt, be necessary to establish an extraterritorial regime for the Christian sacred sites, and to vest their possession and control in an international commission, to which French, on behalf of the Catholic Church, and Russia, on behalf of the Greek Church, would have the leading voices. It would be desirable also that the Mohammedan sacred sites should be declared inviolable, and probably that the Governor's council should include one or more Mohammedans, whose presence would be a guarantee that Mohammedans interests would be safe-guarded...

The British Empire, with its present vastness and prosperity, has little addition to its greatness left to win...the inclusion of Palestine within the British Empire would add a lustre even to the British Crown...

But to strip Germany of her colonies for the benefit of England would leave a permanent feeling of such intense bitterness among the German people as to render such a course impolitic. We have to live in the same world with 70,000,000 Germans, and we should take care to give as little justification as we can for the hatching, ten, twenty, or thirty years hence, of a German war of revenge...

The course which is advocated would win for England the lasting gratitude of the Jews throughout the world..."

Scene 7

Margot Asquith and her husband are served a glass of wine at 10 Downing Street in the fall of 1916.

ASQUITH: I can't believe he is gone-- a force as mighty as Kitchener silenced by the sea.

MARGOT: At some point, historians must scrutinize the influence of the press on political decisions. The right to have an opinion is one thing; to purposefully distort the truth is another.

ASQUITH (silently gazes into space): This war has never made any sense.

MARGOT: First, Lloyd George went after Lord Kitchener and now he and his friends in the press will force us out.

ASQUITH: I'm afraid that the loss of Raymond has made my supervision of this war unbearable. My own son dies in an insane war which I know will accomplish exactly nothing.

MARGOT: We share the grief of a million English families.

ASQUITH: I can't get the image out of my mind: Lord Kitchener standing on the bridge of HMS Hampshire. They said he stood erect and saluted as the boat sank beneath the waves. Wouldn't that have been just the way he would go?

MARGOT: He gave his whole life for the Empire, but I didn't think he would die at sea.

ASQUITH: How did the U boats anticipate the route? It was almost as if they were waiting for the Hampshire.

MARGOT: Maybe you have had enough? Have we spent enough time in the public service? Is it time to go home?

ASQUITH: Politicians are like old soldiers-- they never walk away when they should. We are honored to take part in a great discussion, a great historical discussion, and we are here because we believe our voices should guide our nation. I could walk away but then Lloyd George would try to expand the war. I can't let him do that.

MARGOT: Why would he expand the war? Every nation now professes to want peace.

ASQUITH: All this nonsense in the press about administration and supplying bullets and shells is a smoke screen: they won't rest until millions more have died.

MARGOT: For what? What do they hope to accomplish?

ASQUITH: The public narrative has gotten away from us. We are no longer just waging a war against the Germans; we are waging a war against factions in our own country. They don't want more efficient administration of the war; they want different aims, different goals. They want to conquer Palestine.

MARGOT: Palestine? What advantage is there to the conquest of Palestine? The Germans aren't in Palestine.

ASQUITH: The war against the Germans cannot be won. We have been in opposing trenches for the last 2 years. There has been no movement, but rather than make a humanitarian peace, they secretly scheme for Palestine. Haldane recognized this. He knew we should quit the war with no change in boundaries. They pressured him out.

MARGOT: We will be next.

ASQUITH: That's right. The newspapers have wriggled their way into the diplomatic process. Lloyd George uses them to embarrass us and push his own agenda.

MARGOT: Lloyd George can't believe the war might be won.

ASQUITH: He does. The Zionists claim that they will be able to get the Americans into the war. If the British support a Jewish homeland in Palestine, they claim they will be able to recruit the Americans.

MARGOT: The Americans don't want to be in the war. They just re-elected President Wilson. His entire campaign was to stop the war. He calls himself a "friend of humanity." The Americans are not going to fight for the Zionists.

ASQUITH: Right. Wilson has kept the country neutral as he promised that he would.

MARGOT: How can they be so sure that the Americans will enter the war?

ASQUITH: I can't imagine that it is possible. As ridiculous as it would be to have English boys dying in an invasion of Palestine, it would be even more absurd to have Americans dying in France.

What business do the Americans have in France? No American mother would let her son die in France for the British Empire.

MARGOT: The press published stories about German atrocities. That's how they sold the war here.

ASQUITH: Civilization was never grander than in the early summer of 1914: from St. Petersburg to Vienna; from Berlin to Paris to London stretched the most refined civilization in all of history. How could this have happened?

MARGOT: President Wilson won the election and I don't see why he will change his mind. Americans have no business trying to settle a European war. European leaders have made peace treaties for all previous wars: they should end this war..

ASQUITH: Indeed, we should. Rather than posture further, the leaders of the great countries should stop this war and prevent further slaughter. An entire generation has died over a misunderstanding. The great evil here is not Germany; the great evil here is the idea that civilized men should kill each other to resolve disputes. War should be permanently banned, as Wilson says. There is no excuse for war.

Scene 8

Armenian diplomat JAMES MALCOLM enters the office of Sir Mark Sykes in the Foreign Office in the winter of 1916.

MALCOLM: Cheer up, Sir Mark. Does the war have you down?

SYKES: The war is not going well, I'm afraid.

MALCOLM: How so?

SYKES: The boys can't advance from the trenches in France; Gallipoli was a failure; and we had to surrender in Mesopotamia.

MALCOLM: Our blockade at sea surely must be starving the Germans.

SYKES: Actually, the Germans had a good harvest this year and it is their blockade of us, courtesy of their U boats, that is causing trouble. We're not winning this war.

MALCOLM: Why don't you get the Americans into the war?

SYKES: We've tried. They want to stay neutral. They don't see a reason why American boys should face the German machine guns and poison gas. You must remember that many Americans trace their origins to Germany.

MALCOLM: There is a certain way to get the Americans to join.

SYKES: Do you believe there is?

MALCOLM: The Jews in America are very well positioned. Harry Sacher tells me that they own the most influential newspapers.

SYKES: We've tried to work with the American Jews. They make up a small part of the population.

MALCOLM: What special consideration have you offered them?

SYKES: Special consideration?

MALCOLM: What have you offered the Jews to help get America into the war?

SYKES: The benefit of supporting the victors of this war, assuming we are the victors.

MALCOLM: You must offer them Palestine.

SYKES: Palestine?

MALCOLM: Have you heard of the Zionist movement, Sir Mark?

SYKES: I know that Harry Sacher opposes it. Lord Edwin Montagu is against it and his cousin Herbert Samuel favors it. The Jews here can't decide if they want it or oppose it.

MALCOLM: You deal with only the very affluent Jews. The real Jews, the poor immigrants from Russia, strongly favor Zionism.

SYKES: Is that so?

MALCOLM: If you were to offer to help the Zionists re-establish a Jewish homeland in Palestine, they would bring the Americans into the war.

SYKES: I don't see how that is possible.

MALCOLM: Who have you approached?

SYKES: I know the Chief Rabbi, Moses Gaster.

MALCOLM: Then you have been speaking to the wrong Jews.

SYKES: The Chief Rabbi is not the right Jew?

MALCOLM: Would you like to meet the most dynamic Zionist Jew in England?

SYKES: Who might that be?

MALCOLM: There is a Russian chemist-- Chaim Weizmann-- who works for David Lloyd George. If you get to know Dr. Weizmann, he will share a vision of Zionism you have never heard before. He is the Jew you must meet.

SYKES: I'm open to meeting anyone who can help us win the war.

MALCOLM: Then he is your man. Will you allow me to arrange a meeting with him?

SYKES: Yes. I will run it by some of my supervisors in the Foreign Office, but yes, a meeting does no one any harm.

MALCOLM: This is an historic day, Sir Mark. You will soon meet a man who can change everything.

Scene 9

Woodrow Wilson and his wife Edith speak with Colonel House in the White House early in January 1917 following Wilson's recent re-election. Colonel House recently returned from Europe.

WILSON: You specifically told him that "England is the only obstacle to peace?"

HOUSE: Those were the exact words that I used.

WILSON: Do the British understand that I feel obligated to do what I can to end this senseless conflict?

HOUSE: I don't know how I could have been more specific.

WILSON: "I am the only person in high authority amongst all the peoples of the world at liberty to speak and hold nothing back." I can speak for Americans and "for friends of humanity in every nation."

EDITH: You have an obligation to speak against the sin of war, dear.

WILSON: We have asked them to state their "basic aims." We were ignored.

HOUSE: Lord Lansdowne's memo was received well by the gentry but rejected by the press. He calls for an end to the madness and a resumption of previous borders. His memo is essentially the same position put forward in the German war note. The nations are much closer to peace than anyone understands.

WILSON: Quite right. In truth, permanent peace cannot be achieved by one nation imposing terms on another nation. "Only a peace between equals can last."

HOUSE: We now stand at a point where loyal and experienced Englishman call for peace based on previous borders and the leadership of Germany offers essentially the same language. Almost every nation in the war sees the way to peace and the key to the peace is not fighting to the bitter end; it is to recognize that humanity is best served by an end to the murder and a negotiation of the details.

WILSON: "Victory would mean peace forced upon the loser, a victor's terms imposed upon the vanquished. It would be accepted in humiliation, under duress..."

HOUSE: The fault here is war itself. We should figure out a way to permanently avoid war.

WILSON: The idea that we can simply move people from one land to another makes no sense. "No right anywhere exists to hand peoples about from sovereignty to sovereignty as if they were property." "These are American principles...They are the principles of mankind and must prevail."

HOUSE: Your idea to have America create a "League for Peace" will change the thinking in Europe, but I don't know how long the Germans can resist answering the British embargo of the seas without an embargo of their own. The British have a blockade and the Germans feel that the British should either end their blockade and end the war or understand that the Germans must increase their blockade. The Germans have proposed a reasonable peace; the British should either make peace or expect a more punitive blockade to bring them to the bargaining table.

WILSON: We must make the "keystone of the settlement arch the future security of the world against wars, and letting territorial adjustments be subordinate to the main purpose."

HOUSE: This should put an end to colonialism. The whole point is that we wouldn't have wars of rebellion if people could run their own countries.

WILSON: Yes. Every nation should recognize that there is a "right of nations to determine under what government they should continue to live."

EDITH: A peace without victory, Woodrow.

WILSON: Exactly. We must have "a peace without victory." This victory will be to create a world that is stable, and where nations meet together, and never again make war.

HOUSE: We know what we need to do, Mr. President. We need to put an end to secret treaties. We need to base the peace "on open covenants for peace, openly arrived at," not the secret intrigues of the old world.

WILSON: I will go to the Senate and convince them of the logic of pursuing peace rather than pursuing war.

Scene 10

James Malcolm leads Chaim Weizmann to see Sir Mark Sykes at the Foreign Office on January 28, 1917. Sykes stands as Malcolm leads Weizmann toward his desk.

MALCOLM: Sir Mark, I'd like for you to meet Dr. Chaim Weizmann.

The two men who are approximately of the same tall stature stare at each other for a long moment as they shake hands.

SYKES: Welcome, Dr. Weizmann. I've heard you are the most important Zionist in England.

WEIZMANN: I'm from Russia as you know.

SYKES: So, I have heard, but you have been working with our munitions division for Prime Minister Lloyd George.

WEIZMANN: Yes, and I've met many of the Zionists in England and many of the anti-Zionists.

SYKES: Could you excuse us for a few minutes, Mr. Malcolm?

Malcolm looks around for an uncomfortable moment and then leaves the office.

SYKES: Please sit down.

WEIZMANN: I appreciate your interest in Zionism.

SYKES: To be clear, I have no interest in Zionism. I have an interest and a duty to win this war.

WEIZMANN: I have an un-sworn duty to re-establish a Jewish commonwealth in Palestine.

SYKES: The question I have for you is what you offer that is new? We have talked about a proposal for more than a year. Mr. Malcolm believes the idea originated with him but that's only because he does not have my job.

WEIZMANN: I don't mind if Mr. Malcolm takes the credit for coming up with the idea. In some ways, that would be better.

SYKES: It would be if this meeting were ever to become publicly known, but it won't be; so, it doesn't make any difference who claims credit for the idea. What makes you believe that an agreement can be reached? What do you offer?

WEIZMANN: I can bring the Americans into the war.

SYKES: In return for British Empire recognition of a Jewish home in Palestine.

WEIZMANN: That's the offer.

The two men stare at each other for another long moment.

SYKES: What makes you believe that the Americans want to enter the war?

WEIZMANN: They don't. They don't want to enter the war-- yet. Their president was recently re-elected based on staying out of the war and he made a speech only last week in the Senate where he called for "peace without victory."

SYKES: A new concept in the annals of warfare, I believe.

WEIZMANN (smiling): Yes. Probably so.

SYKES: With President Wilson against the war, what makes you believe you can bring the Americans in?

WEIZMANN: Former President Roosevelt recently called Wilson "yellow" and agitates for American entry.

SYKES: Roosevelt is out of power.

WEIZMANN: There are certain leaders who favor American intervention.

SYKES: I'm sure there are.

WEIZMANN: We have connections to President Wilson's closest advisors. They are positioned to influence his judgment. We also have some friends in the American press. If the American newspapers were to sell the war to the public, as they did here in England, President Wilson would be more inclined to enter the war.

SYKES: He might be. What issue will the American press use to sell the public?

WEIZMANN: The Germans have recently started unrestricted U boat warfare.

SYKES: Yes, but the British have been imposing a blockade on the Germans for the last two years. That headline has already been used. What if the American public believes that the British should end the war based on Lord Lansdowne's proposal-- a proposal which was echoed in the German war note?

WEIZMANN: Obviously, forces for peace are moving on both sides. The war has been a stalemate for the last two years, so the only way to win the war is to bring in the Americans. The only other choice would be a negotiated settlement which sounds like it could be imminent.

SYKES: Is there another issue you might use?

WEIZMANN: Isn't it true, Sir Mark, that you run an intelligence operation here in the Foreign Office?

SYKES: If you can call it an intelligence operation, I suppose that is true. I have been part of secret negotiations I can't reveal even to you.

WEIZMANN: What if British intelligence were to come up with a new headline? What if they found something that threatened the American public? What if the American press then used that news to promote intervention? You would get your American allies and the Zionists would get the promise of a home in Palestine.

SYKES: I'm listening. Do you have people in the United States who could help us sell a war to the press?

WEIZMANN: I am in communication with a secret organization in the United States that is idealistic but pragmatically effective. They believe in Zionism and they have organized themselves to do something about it.

SYKES: I know nothing of such an organization.

WEIZMANN: Let's say that a very high American official is positioned to assist us. Assume that the President knows this official rather well.

SYKES (considers): All right. Let's say there is such a person.

WEIZMANN: The Zionists want a home in Palestine.

SYKES: We don't control Palestine.

WEIZMANN: Yes, but you could.

SYKES: That's right. With some effort we could.

WEIZMANN: If the Americans enter the war before summer, then it is agreed that we have performed on our end of the contract and the British would be obligated to issue a public statement favoring a Jewish home in Palestine. If America stays out of the war, you owe us nothing.

SYKES: We have made efforts to get the Americans to enter.

WEIZMANN: Yes, you have, but they are still neutrals and their president speaks in favor of a peace.

SYKES: So, it's a simple contract.

WEIZMANN: It's a simple contract.

SYKES: We don't conduct this war in a vacuum: naturally, we would need to get the approval of some other parties.

WEIZMANN: The French.

SYKES: Yes, the French. Ideally, I'd like to get the Russians to agree to the proposal--maybe even the Vatican.

WEIZMANN: I'm not sure how long the Russians will be represented by their current government, so this is not a contract between the Zionists and the Russians or the Zionists and the French. We are happy to talk to the French. We are happy to send a representative to the Pope, but the deal we have is with the British. Is that understood?

SYKES: Yes, I believe we understand each other. This is a deal between the Zionists and the British Empire.

WEIZMANN: The phrasing of the agreement will be that if we apply the weight of international Jewish influence in favor of the Allies, the British will recognize a Jewish home in Palestine. That's how it will be discussed, but what you want is American entry into the war. Either we can deliver that, or we cannot.

SYKES (rising from his chair): I will need to discuss this at the highest levels here in the Foreign Office. There will be skeptics.

WEIZMANN (rising from his chair): I will need to discuss it with the Zionist leadership. Taking sides in the world war might endanger Jews in Germany. We'll need to consider that risk.

SYKES: Yes. There are risks for us as well.

WEIZMANN: I see your risk as limited.

SYKES: It is, yes, but if the Americans do enter the war, we will be obligated to capture Palestine.

WEIZMANN: And issue a public statement in favor of British support for the Jewish homeland.

SYKES: We could not sign a public document for this agreement.

WEIZMANN: No. It is strictly a gentlemen's agreement between you and me.

SYKES: I'd like to meet with you again soon, perhaps in a more discrete setting, and I'd like to speak with the other Zionists. I will be the only representative of the British government with whom you discuss this arrangement and I will meet your group as a private citizen-- not as a representative of the Empire. Obviously, this agreement depends totally on secrecy.

WEIZMANN: It will only work if it remains a secret.

SYKES: I think we might have an understanding, Dr. Weizmann. It's not an arrangement we can discuss openly but I believe we have the basis of an agreement.

Scene 11

A meeting on 7 February 1917, WALTER ROTHSCHILD, Herbert Samuel, NAHUM SOKOLOW, MOSES GASTER, Chaim Weizmann and Samuel Landman are meeting at Gaster's home in London while Sir Mark Sykes speaks with Harry Sacher in the next room.

WEIZMANN: If we hold out for a Palestine only for Jews, it will mean that the British must take responsibility for removing all the current population.

SOKOLOW: Wouldn't it be much better to simply have the British guarantee a government which allows Jews to enter Palestine and legally buy property?

WEIZMANN: Why settle for that if the British will remove the Palestinians for us?

SOKOLOW: Why push our luck?

SAMUEL: Gentlemen. Let us focus on the bigger question of whether this is at last what we really want for Zionism. We are a small group of Jews making plans to acquire Palestine in a secret agreement with a government that doesn't own Palestine. No court would claim that there is any legal basis for this plan.

WEIZMANN: Are you saying that no agreement we make tonight can be considered a legal agreement?

LANDMAN: There is certainly no precedent for this.

SOKOLOW: We are committed to re-establishing a homeland for the Jewish people. That is why we are here. We can't doubt our goal if we are to be successful in this negotiation.

WALTER ROTHSCHILD: Do we want it said that a small group of Jews gathered and conspired to take Palestine from the people who have lived there for the last 18 centuries?

SOKOLOW: Some would call this a "cabal." News of this would reinforce a stereotype we've battled for a very long time.

WALTER ROTHSCHILD: Do we believe that "international Jewry," as they refer to us, has the power to bring America into the war? Do we possess the power to influence the American choice?

SAMUEL: This is not the time to doubt our power and it is not the time to suggest to the British that we lack the power to do what we are contracting to do. If we can't deliver on our end of the bargain, they won't deliver on their end and this meeting will turn out to have been a false hope.

LANDMAN: We have the power. Our enemies know that we have the power. It is our friends who don't want to admit that we have the power.

SOKOLOW: What power is it? We have the power to encourage some members of the American press to favor war: maybe some writers, some editors, some publishers. Maybe we place some stories? What kind of power is that? We have no army.

SAMUEL: We have some friends in the press and we also have some friends in positions of influence. This agreement opens the door for Jews to return to Palestine. That's all. We still don't know if we will be able to attract Jews to return. They want to go to New York and California.

(Sykes and Sacher begin to return to the main group.)

SOKOLOW: Remember, this opportunity has been centuries in the making.

WEIZMANN: Let's work toward an agreement. We can think through the ethical conflicts later.

(Sykes re-joins the discussion.)

SYKES: After the discussions I had previously with Dr. Weizmann and the discussions I've had here tonight, I believe that we have something concrete. To be clear, His Majesty's Government is not seeking simply the good will or best wishes of the Jewish community. We have been told that there are good reasons to believe that with the help of some pragmatic Jews in America, a secret group with powerful connections, America can be brought into the war. That's what I have been told. That is what I have discussed at the highest levels with my government.

WEIZMANN: Yes, and we have been told that in return for our actions on behalf of the British Empire, in the form of bringing a powerful ally into the war, the British government will announce sympathy for a Jewish homeland in Palestine; and, we agree that the British government will facilitate such a homeland as best as politics allows.

SYKES: Do we agree on the basic outline of the agreement?

The men around the circle nod their heads.

SOKOLOW: Are we to acknowledge that the exact form of the Jewish commonwealth in Palestine is not yet determined?

SYKES: That is understood.

WEIZMANN: Are we agreed that it will be under British protection?

SYKES: We are agreed that other allies must be allowed to come to terms with this agreement. We should not alienate our French or Russian allies. My expectation is that in England and France, this agreement should energize Zionist efforts to support the war; in Russia, the agreement should encourage Zionist efforts to keep the Russians in the war; in Germany, the agreement should encourage Zionist Jews to disrupt the war effort; and in the United States, the agreement should encourage Zionists to support entry into the war.

WEIZMANN: We do not certify that the Russians will stay in the war, nor that the German war effort will be significantly thwarted by Zionist disruption.

SYKES: Without American entry into the war, this gentlemen's agreement becomes meaningless.

WEIZMANN: That is our understanding.

LANDMAN: It is "a *quid pro quo* contract."

SYKES: My friends, let us lift a glass to this agreement. Tomorrow, at the request of Dr. Weizmann, I will authorize your access to British diplomatic communications so that news of this agreement can be transmitted to influential Zionists throughout the world.

(They toast the agreement.)

Act III

Scene 1

Supreme Court Associate Justice Louis Brandeis walks with President Woodrow Wilson outside White House on February 10, 1917.

BRANDEIS: You must quit thinking of yourself as just an American president. At this moment, you are speaking for people throughout the world.

WILSON: Yes, I believe that I see an opportunity for peace for all time: a community of nations whose founding principle is the elimination of war.

BRANDEIS: A league of nations. A united nations.

WILSON: Exactly. For thousands of years, tribes and the governments that coalesced around tribes and ethnic groups have fought each other over land: which race or ethnic group will rule over a boundary? That is outdated now. Now we have trade between countries. We have learned that the true wealth of nations is based not on who administers the land but on international trade.

BRANDEIS: Others do not yet recognize that opinion.

WILSON: No, I suppose not, but with proper leadership, the peoples of the world would agree because the cost of war is too much for a society to bear. Civilized people ask their young men to pick up arms and kill the young men of other countries-- and they call it honor, they call it duty, but it is a sin to kill another man.

BRANDEIS: I understand that but what do we do with people like the Germans who now have threatened to sink our ships going to England and France?

WILSON: We are neutrals; we have been neutrals; we should stay as neutrals.

BRANDEIS: The Germans are breaking the rules of war: they are interfering with international trade. Should laws not apply to all nations?

WILSON: The British have maintained their blockade of the sea routes to Germany for the last two years. If the Germans enforce their blockade of England and France the way that they themselves have been blockaded, perhaps the English will finally come to the bargaining table and make peace and this terrible aberration of civilization will finally come to an end.

BRANDEIS: If war comes to an end with the Germans defeating the British, as their unrestricted U boat policy will surely do, we will end the cycle of war with a German victory.

WILSON: It will be a settlement and it will produce a peace among equals. The Germans and the English and the French will agree to a community of nations-- an international forum-- to prevent wars like this from ever happening again.

BRANDEIS: Why should they? You will have no voice at the table of any post war agreement. We are not in the war.

WILSON: Don't you believe that the countries of Europe will listen to voices of reason regardless of where they are based?

BRANDEIS: Not necessarily, but if we were to demand that they stop their unrestricted submarine warfare, they would be forced to make peace and it would be on your terms.

WILSON: The Germans recently asked for peace in December. They are only enforcing their blockade because the British are starving them of food.

BRANDEIS: Lord Lansdowne agreed that no gain was to be taken from the war itself.

WILSON: It is important that the public not believe we want any advantage of territory from our involvement in the war.

BRANDEIS: No, of course not. You can't be seen to be sending American men to fight a war for territorial gain for the British.

WILSON: We have held the principled position that war is fundamentally the wrong answer to solve problems of boundaries or of migration of people from one nation to another.

BRANDEIS: You are the most principled leader in the world today, but I fear that more and more of our citizens believe that stronger leadership-- leadership unafraid to face up to the German demands-- might be necessary in these troubled times.

WILSON: Stronger leadership? Let me assure you that I do not fear the Germans, I fear the slaughter of young men.

BRANDEIS: If it is a war to end all wars and establish a new world government, then intervention might become our duty to civilization.

WILSON: I have never shirked duty or responsibility.

BRANDEIS: That is your reputation-- although you dodged a bullet during the campaign.

WILSON(smiles): If that story had broken, we might not be here today.

BRANDEIS: Such ridiculous nonsense, isn't it? We focus on issues of war and peace, but the public is intrigued with details of your sexual relations. It really isn't any of their business.

WILSON: Except that they deserve to have a leader who is pure. I made a simple mistake, that's all. I'm sorry about Ellen but Edith was generous enough to forgive me for my transgression.

BRANDEIS: She forgave you, but your friends were able to keep it out of the papers. Those Republicans did everything but take out advertisements that you have a mistress.

WILSON: I appreciate your loyalty.

BRANDEIS: I know you do. I'm glad we were able to help.

WILSON: To her credit, Mary did not release the letters.

BRANDEIS: No, but it was important that her mortgage got paid off and she received a necessary loan.

WILSON: I wonder if I should send more Justice Department agents over to her apartment to seize the letters.

BRANDEIS: No, don't do anything like that. The election is over, and we need to focus on making the right choices for the future. Teddy Roosevelt was right: the public can't imagine you "as a Romeo." He thinks you were naturally cast to be a drugstore clerk. Maybe the pharmacist.

WILSON: I have no interest in changing that perception.

BRANDEIS: Certainly not, but politics is a funny business, isn't it? Some of the people who have been able to help us in the press agree with Roosevelt that we should fulfill our duty in the European war.

WILSON: I've struggled with what to do about Europe.

BRANDEIS: As have we all. Even Walter Lippmann at the New Republic recently has changed his mind about the war. He has been one of your most important friends.

WILSON: Walter Lippmann? Even Walter Lippmann favors war?

BRANDEIS: From what I hear.

WILSON: I hate the thought of sending American youth into the machine guns and the gas of the European trenches. The truth is that it is not our war. Why should I ask young Americans to fight people who are not threatening us?

BRANDEIS: It is a threat. If the Germans can press the English to settle the war, it is likely it will be settled on terms which are not favorable to us.

WILSON: I am a son of the South. I know the horrors of war and I do not favor resolving disputes with violent means.

Scene 2

Sir Mark Sykes sits with Chaim Weizmann in the Foreign Office in February 1917.

WEIZMANN: I am told by Justice Brandeis that President Wilson prefers a negotiated settlement and he is against the idea of moving people from one country to the next.

SYKES: I'm sure Brandeis has not shared our entire agreement with the president.

WEIZMANN: Brandeis supported Wilson in the campaign of 1912-- before he embraced Zionism. In fact, some Americans believe that Brandeis became an ardent Zionist because Wilson did not ask him to be in the cabinet after the 1912 election.

SYKES: Why would Brandeis believe that becoming a Zionist would make him more attractive for a political appointment?

WEIZMANN: One of the senior Jews in New York thought Brandeis wasn't fully "representative of Jews." He lacked political punch.

SYKES: Did becoming an active Zionist gave him political punch?

WEIZMANN: Brandeis traveled around the country selling the ideas of Horace Kallen-- the same young man who suggested the public announcement for a Jewish home in Palestine. Kallen believes that being a Zionist does not conflict with being an

American. A Jew can be loyal to both if the values that both governments pursue are the same.

SYKES: Interesting idea.

WEIZMANN: It made Brandeis the most recognized Jew in the United States. When the Supreme Court spot opened, Brandeis was in line for the appointment.

SYKES: That puts him very close to the president.

WEIZMANN: That's right. And Mr. Brandeis has continued to support President Wilson on many levels.

SYKES: I see.

WEIZMANN: Before he learned about Kallen's ideas, Brandeis thought that serving the interests of another foreign country inevitably introduced Jews to the charge of "dual loyalty." Kallen showed him that if the countries had the same philosophical goals, there would not be dual loyalty.

SYKES: Mr. Kallen markets his ideas well.

WEIZMANN: Kallen's organization of strongly Zionist Jews operates completely in secret. Every editor they contact, every congressman they support, every speaker they heckle knows nothing about their secret organization.

SYKES: Does Mr. Brandeis socialize with the president?

WEIZMANN: Very little. Brandeis understands that people expect justices of the Supreme Court to be above politics, but rumors are that he has been quite helpful to Mr. Wilson.

SYKES: How so?

WEIZMANN: I'm sure you hear the same rumors that I do.

SYKES: Yes, we've heard some of the same rumors. We don't have spies in the United States, like the Germans do, but we have people who send us information. I've learned more in recent weeks.

WEIZMANN: Then surely you know that there were rumors about President Wilson during the election.

SYKES: About a woman?

WEIZMANN: Yes, the Republicans conducted a terrible whisper campaign against the president.

SYKES: Mary Hulbert?

WEIZMANN: You know her name: Mary Allen Hulbert.

SYKES: Formerly, Mary Allen Hulbert Peck. Yes. I've recently learned that Wilson wrote many letters to a woman he met on a vacation. Apparently started before he was governor. Many years; many letters.

WEIZMANN: She kept the letters.

SYKES: Meeting a woman on a vacation in Bermuda, spending time with her, meeting again on the same island every year, and writing hundreds of letters over seven years doesn't suggest innocence.

WEIZMANN: The American public expects the national leadership to be honest. President Wilson carries the reputation of a minister. He walks and speaks with his father's reputation.

SYKES: Some payments were made.

WEIZMANN: That's right and the letters are not yet released.

SYKES: If the letters were completely innocent, Mrs. Hulbert could simply release them to the public.

WEIZMANN: That would not have been favorable to the President.

SYKES: Have you heard who helped President Wilson?

WEIZMANN: I heard some influence was brought to bear, yes. Someone had influence with the larger papers and was able to assist with helping Mrs. Peck.

SYKES: We heard it was Mr. Brandeis.

WEIZMANN: That's who the Republicans named. No proof.

SYKES: Now we've heard that Mr. Brandeis is running Mr. Kallen's secret organization.

WEIZMANN: All rumors. Nothing has been published.

SYKES: Rumors, yes; rumors, indeed.

(Admiral WILLIAM REGINALD HALL enters Sir Mark's office with papers in hand.)

HALL: Sir Mark, I think I've found some communications we might go over.

SYKES: Great news! What do you have?

HALL (looking at Weizmann): Do you want to go over the documents now?

SYKES: Dr. Weizmann, why don't you excuse Admiral Hall and me for this discussion.

(Weizmann rises, shakes hands with Mark Sykes and Admiral Hall, and leaves the room.)

HALL: Ordinarily, I don't discuss Room 40 operations with anyone outside the government.

SYKES: No worry.

HALL: We intercepted several telegrams from the Germans to their ambassador in Mexico a few weeks ago.

SYKES: How do you intercept these messages?

HALL: We cut the German cables, as you know, at the start of the war. But the American cables to Germany have been left intact to allow President Wilson and the Germans to attempt to find a peaceful solution.

SYKES: Right.

HALL: The Americans allow the Germans to use their cable to communicate with their own diplomats in the United States. From there, the Germans use publicly available cable services over land.

SYKES: Yes.

HALL: Even the American cables go through a relay station in England before they go out under the Atlantic. When we boost their power, we also divert the signal to our own boys for private examination.

SYKES: You are a clever lot!

HALL: I believe I've found one transmission which might serve our purposes rather well.

SYKES: Yes...

HALL: It is from the German Foreign Minister to the German ambassador in Mexico City. It instructs the ambassador to reach out to the Mexican government if the Americans decide to enter the war.

SYKES: Is that such a radical idea? If a country is going into a war, wouldn't their diplomats be expected to make contingency plans?

HALL: We're not here to defend the Germans, Sir Mark. What if we released the cable but left out the part about "if the Americans were to enter the war?" What if we just said that the cable was an offer to the Mexican government to become allies with the Germans-- to make it appear that the Germans were currently conspiring with the Mexicans to invade the United States?

SYKES: It must be a credible idea, Hall. The Mexicans would never invade the United States. That's ludicrous. Have you visited that country?

HALL: It's not a question of whether the Mexicans would invade. Of course, they would not invade the United States. It's a question of whether a perception of disloyalty could be suggested. I think Americans might feel more threatened if they believed the Germans might invade from Mexico.

SYKES: I read just the other day that the Americans were trying to see who might be allied with them if they were to declare a war with Germany. Making contingency plans for a war is expected of the foreign service.

HALL: What something says and how it is reported are two different ideas, Sir Mark. We have a cable. Should we share it with the Americans?

SYKES: We have some connections with a group in America that says it can influence the press. Maybe we will see what they are able to do.

Scene 3

Senator GEORGE NORRIS, <u>Proceedings of the United States Senate</u>, April 4, 1917.

NORRIS: "...I am bitterly opposed to my country entering the war, but if, notwithstanding my opposition, we do enter it, all of my energy and all of my power will be behind our flag in carrying it on to victory...No close student of history will deny that both Great Britain and Germany have, on numerous occasions since the beginning of the war, flagrantly violated in the most serious manner the rights of neutral vessels and neutral nations under existing international law...The reason given by the President in asking Congress to declare war against Germany is that the German Government has declared certain war zones, within which, by the use of submarines, she sinks, without notice, American ships and destroys American lives...The first war zone was declared by Great Britain. She gave us and the world notice of it on the 4th day of November 1914. The zone became effective November 5, 1914, the next day after notice was given...The first German war zone was declared on the 4th day of February 1915, just three months after the British war zone was declared. Germany gave 15 days' notice...The British Admiralty gave notice that vessels would be exposed to the gravest danger from mines...The German government...declared that the order would be made effective by use of submarines. Thus we have two declarations of the two governments, each declaring a military zone and warning neutral shipping from going into the prohibited area...Both of these orders were illegal and contrary to all international law as well as the principles of humanity...It is sufficient to say that our government has officially declared both of them to be illegal and has officially protested against both of them...The only difference is that in the case of Germany we have persisted in our protest, while in the case of England we have submitted....We might have refused to permit the sailing of any ship from any American port to either of these military zones. In my judgment, if we had pursued this course, the zones would have been of short duration. England would have been compelled to take her mines out of the North Sea in order to get any supplies from our country....Through this instrumentality and also through the instrumentality of others who have not only made millions out of the war in the manufacture of munitions, etc., and who would expect to make millions more if our country can be drawn into the catastrophe, a large number of the great newspapers and news agencies of the country have been controlled and enlisted in the greatest propaganda that the world has ever known, to manufacture sentiment in favor of war...To whom does the war bring prosperity? Not to the soldier who for the munificent compensation of $16 per month shoulders his musket and goes into the trench, there to shed his blood and die if necessary...War brings no prosperity to the great mass of common and patriotic citizens...We are taking a step to-day that is fraught with untold danger. We are going into war upon the command of gold...I feel that we are committing a sin against humanity and against our countrymen. I would like to say to this war God, you shall not coin into gold the lifeblood of my brethren...This war craze has robbed us of our judgment. I have no more sympathy with the submarine policy of Germany than I have with mine laying policy of England...Let Europe solve her problems as we have solved ours...Upon the passage of this resolution we will have joined Europe in the great catastrophe and taken America into entanglements that will not end with this war, but will live and bring their evil influences upon many generations yet unborn."

Scene 4

James Malcolm, <u>Origins of the Balfour Declaration</u>, London, 1944, published by the British Museum.

MALCOLM: "During one of my visits to the War Cabinet Office in Whitehall Gardens in the late autumn of 1916, I found Sir Mark Sykes less buoyant than usual...He spoke of military deadlock in France, the growing menace of submarine warfare, the unsatisfactory situation which was developing in Russia, and the general bleak outlook...The cabinet was looking anxiously for United States intervention. I asked him what progress was being made in that direction. He shook his head glumly. "Precious little", he replied. He had thought of enlisting the substantial Jewish influence in the United States but had been unable to do so. Reports from America revealed a very pro-German tendency among the wealthy American Jewish bankers and bond issuing houses, nearly all of German origin, and among Jewish journalists who took their cue from them...I enquired what special argument or consideration had the Allies put forward to win over American Jewry...I said to him, "you are going the wrong way about it..." "You can win the sympathy of the Jews everywhere, in one way only, and that way is by offering to try to secure Palestine for them."

"I recounted the gist of my several conversations with Sir Mark Sykes and that I had the War Cabinet's authority for my overtures.

Dr. Weizmann was most interested and asked his colleagues for their views. All of them...were very skeptical...But Dr. Weizmann turned to me again and asked if I was really personally convinced that the Government seriously intended to make a promise of Palestine in consideration of the help required from American Jewry, and if I would advise them to accept, and I replied, "yes, most certainly." Whereupon Dr. Weizmann shook hands with me saying, "I accept your advice," and asked when he could meet Sir Mark Sykes....The results of the talk were very satisfactory. The first step was to inform Zionist leaders in all parts of the world of the compact and Sir Mark said they would be given immediate facilities for cables to be sent through the Foreign Office and the War Office. A special detailed message was at once sent to Justice Brandeis in cipher through the Foreign Office....All of these steps were taken with the full knowledge and approval of Justice Brandeis, between whom and Dr. Weizmann there was an active interchange of cables...The work was making satisfactory progress in the Spring of 1917, when the United States entered the War. Sir Mark Sykes was very confident that the promise of the Government would be publicly confirmed very soon...By issuing the declaration the British Government duly carried out-- as I had all along been convinced they would-- its obligation to promise British help for the Jews to obtain Palestine...The consideration for this contract had already been given by the Jews before November 2nd, 1917...In a letter to me, Dr. Weizmann has recognized my initiative in this work..."

Scene 5

Foreign Secretary Arthur Balfour meets with Associate Justice Louis Brandeis over breakfast at a hotel in Washington, D.C. on May 3, 1917.

BALFOUR: We were all surprised by President Wilson's sudden change.

BRANDEIS: Never doubt the power of political activism.

BALFOUR: I was worried when President Wilson called for the European neutrals to join him in breaking off diplomatic relations with Germany and they all refused to follow his lead.

BRANDEIS: So was I, and I think the President was surprised, believing as he does that he is the leader of all nations.

BALFOUR: And a voice for humanity everywhere.

BRANDEIS: The American press was certainly supportive of our cause from the beginning, and when the German cable was finally released, every politician in America was able to see treachery.

BALFOUR: Surprising.

BRANDEIS: The power of the press.

BALFOUR: I read somewhere that an American mob confronted a German man and hanged him to death on the spot for the crime of being German.

BRANDEIS: An unfortunate incident. It might be time to lighten up a bit on the propaganda.

BALFOUR: Don't lighten up too quickly, old man. We have a war to win yet.

BRANDEIS: At least we've sold it. It wasn't clear that President Wilson would agree to ask for a Declaration of War. His heart is more with the peacemakers.

BALFOUR: We were lucky that the Reuter's news organization was willing to report that the German diplomatic message planned an invasion of the United States.

BRANDEIS: It was a clever idea-- but who could have predicted it would work? Americans were outraged to think that the Germans were planning a Mexican invasion against the United States. That it was only a contingency plan to assess support if America declared war against Germany was later clarified but lost in the moment.

BALFOUR: Someone must have a friend over at Reuter's.

BRANDEIS: The news agency apologized but the damage to the Germans was done.

BALFOUR: When do you believe that we can expect American soldiers to arrive in Europe?

BRANDEIS: That might take some time. We lack a standing army. We will need to field an army and equip them. Wilson might take his time doing that.

BALFOUR: We will need some relief from the U boat blockade.

BRANDEIS: I'm sure support will be forthcoming assuming we have your assurance that the British will secure Palestine and, of course, there is the matter of the declaration of support for the Jewish homeland.

BALFOUR: We are committed to both, let me assure you.

BRANDEIS: I'm sure you are but you also must understand that while we helped gather American support for your cause before you voice support for ours, you should continue with our agreement while we are mobilizing to assist you.

BALFOUR: Yes, that is our understanding.

BRANDEIS: I'm sure you know that James de Rothschild cabled me with the question of who should protect Palestine after the war.

BALFOUR: I know the topic has been discussed on our side of the Atlantic.

BRANDEIS: President Wilson stands against imperialism. I'm sure you know that. He favors countries having the right of self-determination.

BALFOUR: That is a position which has made him quite popular in our colonies around the world.

BRANDEIS: He is most sincere in his view.

BALFOUR: I'm sure he is. Disrupting the Turkish Empire goes along with his views on giving people the right to choose their own governments, but I doubt he will want to see the British extend our Empire into the countries released by the Turks.

BRANDEIS: We are not talking about the British ruling Palestine--only a protectorate.

BALFOUR: What is your thought? Would the Americans be willing to serve as the protectors of a Jewish Palestine?

BRANDEIS: I'm afraid not.

BALFOUR: No?

BRANDEIS: No. I discussed the question with the President. He believes that he would be hypocritical to be seen calling for other countries to be able to choose their own governments but require the Palestinians to live under an American government which appears to be taking the country for the Jews.

BALFOUR: It's going to be a tricky transition.

BRANDEIS: I would say so.

BALFOUR: Less than 10% of the population of Palestine is currently Jewish. No government is going to look noble by supervising the transition of ownership of land from one people to another.

BRANDEIS: The land was owned by the Jews.

BALFOUR: That was almost 18 centuries ago. It's a bit like your American Indians coming back to New York or Washington and claiming that the land was promised to them by God. They have been gone only a century or two at the most.

BRANDEIS: The Jews must have somewhere to go.

BALFOUR: We agree. We have enough Jews in England. Palestine is a logical conclusion if Jews continue to flee Russia. They won't all be able to go to the United States, either.

BRANDEIS: Well, they could. On some days, I wonder if they should. Some of the anti-Zionists in the United States say that the ancient land of Israel is gone forever and that we Zionists are fooling ourselves into thinking that it can somehow be restored. They say that America is the new Zion. Jews are protected by law. We practice our religion without persecution.

BALFOUR: Jews should have a choice. They will need to continue to flee Russia if the Monarchists re-gain control, and they will want to go to Palestine or to America.

BRANDEIS: President Wilson is unwilling to put the United States in a position to support or protect a new Jewish homeland in Palestine, but he has agreed to announce his support for a British protectorate when requested.

BALFOUR: The British Empire has committed itself to supporting a Jewish homeland. It has not been announced but it has been committed. There is still plenty of time for the Americans to become the protectors of the Jewish enterprise.

Scene 6

Sitting in his judicial robes, Associate Justice Louis Brandeis meets with Horace Kallen in his chambers at the United States Supreme Court.

KALLEN: I had nothing to do with how the telegram was leaked or with how it was reported.

BRANDEIS: It should never have been reported as a plan to invade the United States. We're lucky Americans are not turning on the poor Mexican-Americans like they are the innocent German-Americans.

KALLEN: Once we unleashed the forces of propaganda, the story has taken a life of its own.

BRANDEIS: Some of this propaganda is grossly unfair.

KALLEN: We encouraged some writers to report on the leaked cable and some editors to consider implications of the story. No one ever thought it would turn into a lynch mob. The Kaiser has gone from being a king to being a demon.

BRANDEIS: It is appropriate to remember that modern Zionism was an idea from central Europe. We're backing the British, but it could have gone the other way.

KALLEN: It still might.

BRANDEIS: Not really. The Germans would never have agreed to release Palestine from the Ottoman Empire. In the best case, they would have allowed us to buy land there and they wouldn't allow us to make Hebrew the national language.

KALLEN: I just wonder how much those things are worth. Jews who want to speak Hebrew can do it anytime they like. They just want to live in a peaceful country with the rule of law.

BRANDEIS: We can't be seen to be pushing the war.

KALLEN: Obviously not. Who would have thought the New York Times would be the paper that demanded you give up your public leadership of Zionism? Now, I'm glad they did.

BRANDEIS: Right. I'm no longer seen as a public leader promoting the Zionist cause. Fortunately, no one knows about the Parushim.

KALLEN: That's exactly the reason I insisted on keeping the Parushim completely secret.

BRANDEIS: If the public saw a connection between Zionists and American entry into the war--

Felix Frankfurter bursts into the chambers of Justice Brandeis.

FRANKFURTER: --We're in trouble!

BRANDEIS (rising from his chair): What is it?

FRANKFURTER: They are going to try to stop us.

BRANDEIS: Stop what? Try to make sense.

FRANKFURTER: They are going to try to stop the war.

BRANDEIS: Who's going to try to stop the war? The Americans are not yet in the war.

FRANKFURTER: Wilson and Ambassador Morgenthau are up to no good. Morgenthau wants to go to Turkey and make a separate peace with the Turks. If he can get them to drop out of the war, the Germans will make peace.

BRANDEIS: Crazy bastard!

FRANKFURTER: He knows nothing of the secret agreement.

BRANDEIS: Obviously not. He's going to ruin more than two years of negotiations and plans.

KALLEN: If the war could be avoided, we might still get a commitment for the Jews to live in Palestine.

BRANDEIS: Could we make that a condition of the settlement?

KALLEN: We might. If we can re-establish a Jewish commonwealth without a war, so much the better.

BRANDEIS: That's something to think about but we shouldn't take risks. When does Morgenthau leave?

FRANKFURTER: I don't have the details. I just heard the rumor over at the War Department. President Wilson has endorsed the plan.

BRANDEIS: Wilson hasn't endorsed anything. Wilson doesn't know what he's going to do until he speaks to me.

FRANKFURTER: Wilson has agreed to let Morgenthau go talk to Pasha and Bey. He hasn't committed to anything other than talk. If Morgenthau gets the Turks to drop out of the war, the whole thing would be over, and Palestine would still be ruled by the Turks.

BRANDEIS: That isn't going to help us. Who is Morgenthau taking with him?

FRANKFURTER: I have no idea.

BRANDEIS: Good, because he's taking you. I'll speak to President Wilson and find out about this nonsense. In the worst case, you go with Morgenthau as a representative of the War Department and keep an eye on him. We might have to bring him into the circle.

FRANKFURTER: I'm not sure I'm available to go.

BRANDEIS: You're available. I just freed you up from any other obligations. We'll get some of our other boys to go with you. Morgenthau thinks he's going to lead a group to Constantinople, but what he doesn't know is that I will be planning the trip.

FRANKFURTER: Morgenthau is a crazy old Jew who thinks he knows everything.

BRANDEIS: Yes, well he's lucky: he will now meet a crazy old Jew who does know everything. We'll get to Morgenthau. I'll fix this.

Scene 7

HENRY MORGENTHAU, SR., and his party of American Zionists enter the British garrison in Gibraltar on July 5, 1917. Felix Frankfurter, Frankfurter's assistant-- the lawyer MAX LOWENTHAL, and ELIHU LEWIN-EPSTEIN, the treasurer of the Zionist Provisional Executive Committee in New York City, follow Morgenthau. ASHAG SCHMARVONIAN, a Turkish Armenian from the Department of State and the earlier translator for Morgenthau in Turkey, walks with Morgenthau. They are greeted by Chaim Weizmann and surrounded by British soldiers holding weapons. Two French representatives, Colonel E. WEYL and ALBERT THOMAS, are also present.

WEIZMANN: Does everyone here speak French?

WEIZMANN (looks at the raised hands): English?

WEIZMANN: German?

MORGENTHAU: These guards are going to wonder about this meeting if we must conduct it in German.

FRANKFURTER: It's the only language we all know.

WEIZMANN: They'll probably conclude that we are a bunch of spies and shoot us at dawn.

MORGENTHAU: Ashag served me well in Constantinople when I was ambassador there. I thought he should start by telling us about the condition of the Turkish government.

SCHMARVONIAN: The war has been hard on the government of Turkey. The Turks remain allied with Germany but wish to drop out of the war. The cost of fighting the British at Gallipoli was significant and has demanded that the government divert more cash into the war effort. Talaat Pasha and Enver Bey are at each other's throats and there is good reason to believe that they would like a separate peace from Germany.

MORGENTHAU: If the Turks make a separate peace, we could avoid prolonging the war with the savings of life and money that peace would bring.

WEIZMANN: What terms might the Turks be willing to take?

SCHMARVONIAN: Obviously, it is impossible to know what they would accept before negotiations. I suppose it would depend on what would be offered. To drop out of the war would mean that pressure would encourage Germany to negotiate an immediate settlement.

MORGENTHAU: The world is ready for peace. Lord Lansdowne proposed that they all go back to the same borders as existed before the war. That proposal was reflected and endorsed by the German peace proposal of December. I believe all governments have concluded that any advantage gained by war does not justify the terrible loss of life. Europeans are tired of war.

SCHMARVONIAN: The Turks are almost bankrupt. They want to quit.

WEIZMANN: I can't believe the British and the French want to end the war with nothing to show for it.

COLONEL WEYL: The French want peace. Nothing about the borders of Europe or Turkey threatens France.

WEIZMANN: We don't even know what terms the Turks would require.

SCHMARVONIAN: That's the reason Ambassador Morgenthau has initiated this mission. We want to find out.

WEIZMANN: Thank you for your thoughts, Mr. Schmarvonian. I think it is wise to break into smaller discussion groups for the purposes of better understanding Ambassador Morgenthau's idea.

COLONEL WEYL: The people of France want peace and the government of France wants peace. All our government wants is the protection of our commercial interests in the area which I am sure the Turks will be more than happy to accommodate.

WEIZMANN: Not necessarily so, I'm afraid. We will need to find out their terms. Before Ambassador Morgenthau goes on to Constantinople, I would like to speak with him and a few of his party-- for the purposes of discussion. We will share our thoughts after we have had an opportunity to speak. Please excuse us for now.

(The French representatives, Schmarvonian, Lowenthal, and Lewin-Epstein leave the room. Morgenthau, Weizmann, and Felix Frankfurter stay.)

WEIZMANN: Thank you, gentlemen. We will be with you shortly.

MORGENTHAU: Why did they have to leave?

WEIZMANN: We have secret items to discuss.

MORGENTHAU: What secret items do we have? I don't even know you.

WEIZMANN: You do, Ambassador Morgenthau. I am the Russian cousin you never met.

MORGENTHAU: I don't have any Russian cousins.

WEIZMANN: The Russian Jews are different. The Russian Jews understand that governments cannot be trusted. Jews must look out for themselves.

MORGENTHAU: What are you talking about?

WEIZMANN: You are coming to the table quite late, Mr. Ambassador. We have already negotiated an agreement of which you are unaware.

MORGENTHAU: Is it an agreement unknown to President Wilson?

WEIZMANN: He knows what he needs to know. There are secrets which can be publicly leaked and discussed and there are secrets which can never be known.

MORGENTHAU: I'm starting to wonder why I agreed to stop here. Louis Brandeis suggested that I should speak to you, but as I look at your assistants, I see that Brandeis arranged to have you all here. Brandeis wanted this.

WEIZMANN: Brandeis knows the secrets.

MORGENTHAU: He is a judge on the Supreme Court. Why is he even involved in my trip to Turkey?

WEIZMANN: Let me just ask you: what do you hope to accomplish with your visit to Constantinople?

MORGENTHAU: I approached President Wilson with the goal of going to Constantinople to see if I could arrange a peace with the Turkish Empire. I believe they are ready to drop out of the war.

WEIZMANN: Is that your true mission?

MORGENTHAU: Yes, that is my true mission, but I have another goal as well.

WEIZMANN: What is that other goal?

MORGENTHAU: You are a Russian Zionist, aren't you Dr. Weizmann?

WEIZMANN: I am now the leader of the British Zionist Organization in London.

MORGENTHAU: Right, but you don't have any more authority to speak for the Jewish people than I do.

WEIZMANN: Except that I am the President of the British Zionist Organization.

MORGENTHAU: Yes, and therefore you have no more authority to speak for the world's Jews than I do. You represent some Zionists in England. That's all you represent. You don't represent me and I am also a Jew-- but of German descent.

WEIZMANN: I would have never guessed that.

MORGENTHAU: Do you want to know the goals of my mission or do you want to make jokes?

WEIZMANN: What are the goals of your mission-- other than to see if the Turks are willing to state their terms for peace.

MORGENTHAU: I happen to be rather close to the people who are ruling Turkey. I've known Talaat Pasha and Enver Bey since 1912 and I know the situation in the Ottoman Empire. As I say, I represented the government of the United States in Constantinople for almost 4 years.

WEIZMANN: I congratulate you on your service, but you are starting to meddle in a very delicate diplomatic agreement which might have a great impact on the future of the Jewish people.

MORGENTHAU: You too are meddling with a possible diplomatic agreement.

WEIZMANN: Is that so?

MORGENTHAU: Yes, that's so. Out in the harbor is the boat which brought me and my party to Gibraltar. It is carrying 18 trunks of gold. I have $400,000 dollars' worth of gold out in the harbor.

WEIZMANN: I've heard you're a wealthy man.

MORGENTHAU: The money was donated to be a down payment to purchase some property currently controlled by the Ottoman Empire.

WEIZMANN: I see.

MORGENTHAU: The Turks are approaching bankruptcy. They need gold. That's good because I happen to have a lot of gold just outside. The Turks have some land that I would like to buy from them.

WEIZMANN: You want to buy Palestine from the Turks?

MORGENTHAU: Yes, that's right. Before I left Constantinople, I was negotiating to buy a great deal of land controlled by the Ottoman

Empire in Palestine. Now, I am returning with the money to close the deal. Do you have any idea how far $400,000 in gold will go to purchase land in Palestine?

WEIZMANN: I have no idea.

MORGENTHAU: Well, I do have an idea. I have an idea because I was in negotiations with the leaders of the Ottoman Empire before I left. I'm not paying in dollars or in marks. I'm paying in gold.

WEIZMANN: Do you propose to buy Palestine?

MORGENTHAU: I propose to buy a large part of it and I propose to do it from the government which controls it.

WEIZMANN: There is a war in Europe. What makes you think the Ottomans will exist as an empire when the war is over?

MORGENTHAU: If the Ottomans take this gold, the American Zionists who put up this money will own part of the Holy Land. Their ownership will be guaranteed by the Turks if the Turks win and certainly by the Allied powers if the Allied powers win. The general concept here is that we will buy large parts of Palestine from the people who have uncontested title to it. That makes me more of Zionist than you, Dr. Weizmann.

WEIZMANN: You can't buy Palestine for $400,000.

MORGENTHAU: Like I said, I've been in negotiations to do so. The final cost would be more like $4 million, but you must remember that the Americans bought half their country for $15 million a century ago. We will buy vast areas which haven't been farmed in modern times. Desert land is cheap, sir, and there is plentiful desert in Palestine. We're not talking about buying vacation homes.

WEIZMANN: Then you would develop the land.

MORGENTHAU: Of course. We would buy the land as desert and then we would bring water to the desert. We would make the desert bloom. Can you imagine what people might pay to have a home in the Holy Land? This is going to be one of the greatest real estate deals in history.

WEIZMANN: Except for one problem: it isn't ever going to happen.

MORGENTHAU: You say what?

WEIZMANN: Zionists in England have negotiated with the British government for more than a year and a half. We made an agreement.

MORGENTHAU: What's your agreement?

WEIZMANN: The British guaranteed to publicly endorse a homeland for the Jewish people in Palestine.

MORGENTHAU: That's great but it doesn't get you the land. We buy the land from the Turks. We decide who gets to settle on the land.

WEIZMANN: The British will publicly endorse a homeland in Palestine and they will capture Palestine from the Ottoman Empire.

MORGENTHAU: What? You propose that the British should capture Palestine?

WEIZMANN: That is the agreement that we have made with the British.

MORGENTHAU: In return for what? How much are you paying the British for this substantial service?

WEIZMANN: We have already provided the compensation for their support.

MORGENTHAU: With what? How much gold did you pay?

WEIZMANN: Actually, we didn't pay them in gold.

MORGENTHAU: What did you pay them with?

WEIZMANN: We helped them bring in their American allies.

MORGENTHAU: Did I hear you correctly? Did you say that you helped bring America into the war?

WEIZMANN: We organized support for the Allied cause in the United States.

MORGENTHAU: I can't believe what I'm hearing. How were you able to rally American opinion in favor of the war?

WEIZMANN: Let's just say that we have certain connections in the United States that were instrumental in bringing in the Americans.

MORGENTHAU: I'm sorry. I thought I was talking to fellow Jews here. Jews know how to do business. Jews know how to follow the law. You are claiming that you have made a deal with the British Empire to obtain land not owned by the British Empire by secretly nudging the Americans into the war. Is that your claim?

WEIZMANN: We were able to help the British cause in America.

MORGENTHAU: Is that how Russian Jews do business? You contract with one party to seize the property of another party in exchange for secret manipulation of a third party to assist with the war? Do I understand this correctly?

WEIZMANN: Jews have been persecuted under the laws of many countries.

MORGENTHAU: The Jews invented law! What do they teach you in Russia? We are a law-abiding people, loyal to countries where we live. We do not conspire to push countries into war! We believe in law. We worship our faith under the protection of law. Have you thought through the implications of this agreement?

WEIZMANN: Of course, we have thought through the implications.

MORGENTHAU: That's not what I'm hearing. It doesn't sound like anyone has thought this through.

WEIZMANN: We have thought it through.

MORGENTHAU: Really? Let me ask you a few questions. If the British win the war, with the help of the Americans, what happens to the Jews in England and America?

WEIZMANN: They will be encouraged to live in Palestine. A great new Israel will be founded in the ancient land of Palestine.

MORGENTHAU: So, Jews like me will be encouraged by our neighbors to go to the Jewish homeland.

WEIZMANN: No, it would only be intended to give you the choice to go. It would provide a place for you to go if you so wished.

MORGENTHAU: If Jews run into trouble in the lands where they are now living, it is not unreasonable to think that there might be pressures on them to go to Palestine.

WEIZMANN: Anything is possible.

MORGENTHAU: Right-- anything is possible, and given enough time, everything becomes probable. Now let's assume that the British lose the war. Say the Americans can't mobilize an army fast enough or the Germans improve their U boat technology enough to prevent the American Army from getting to Europe. What happens if the Germans find out that Zionists conspired to bring Americans into the war against them. How will that affect the Jews in England and the United States?

WEIZMANN: The Germans will have won the war and Germans are known to meticulously follow their treaties. They will focus on governing the peace.

MORGENTHAU: All right. Maybe the American Jews would be fine if the Germans won the war, but you are going to issue a public endorsement of British support for a Jewish homeland. So, the German Jews who are Zionists will be encouraged to tip the war in Germany in favor of the Allies.

WEIZMANN: We hope that they do tip the war in favor of the Allies. That would be a benefit to the Allies.

MORGENTHAU: Of course, it would. If the Germans lost the war, they might blame the Jews for dual citizenship, divided loyalties. If the Germans lose the war, how will you prevent them from coming to the obvious conclusion that the Jews sold them out?

WEIZMANN: There will be no evidence of Jews hampering the German war effort.

MORGENTHAU: Do you think you can have a public endorsement for a Jewish homeland in Palestine and the Germans will not suspect disloyalty?

WEIZMANN: I'm just saying the help of the German Zionists will not be obvious.

MORGENTHAU: I'm telling you that it couldn't be anything other than obvious. Do you know why I left Constantinople without buying Palestine from the Turks?

WEIZMANN: No, I can't imagine why you would leave if you were in negotiations to buy Palestine.

MORGENTHAU: If you don't know why I left Turkey, you have missed the most important lesson of this insane war. I left because I became aware that the Turks were slaughtering the Armenians.

WEIZMANN: Bad things can occur in war.

MORGENTHAU: They can, indeed. Very bad things can happen behind the cover of war. During 1915, I became aware that Armenians were being killed only for the crime of being Armenian.

WEIZMANN: A great tragedy.

MORGENTHAU: Men, women, and children were slaughtered--- many by sword but many more by machine gun-- and they were buried in pits. Their bodies were burned in pits! The technological advances of warfare in this century astound; and these advances make murder, mass murder, much more likely.

WEIZMANN: The use of poison gas has been introduced in this war.

MORGENTHAU: That's exactly right. Now it will be possible for a soldier to not even see the enemy who takes his life. Poison gas will be dropped on cities. Entire populations will be exterminated.

WEIZMANN: Every citizen should have a gas mask.

MORGENTHAU: Every government should avoid war. War should be unimaginable to any leader. President Wilson's proposal to make the maintenance of peace the keystone in the settlement arch is an idea worthy of a modern prophet. We shouldn't give citizens gas masks; we should go to whatever lengths are necessary to avoid war.

WEIZMANN: I salute your idealism, but we don't live in an ideal world. We must look out for our own.

MORGENTHAU: We must look out for our own and for everyone else's own. We are one world, Dr. Weizmann; one people. Stopping a war today prevents another war in the future. Lasting peace can only be founded on justice.

WEIZMANN: I am sorry to hear about the fate of the Armenians.

MORGENTHAU: Of course, you are sorry; but let me ask you: what started the great genocide of the Armenian people?

WEIZMANN: I assume that the Turks wanted their property.

MORGENTHAU: Yes, I'm sure that some Turks claimed the lost property of the Armenians; but the excuse they gave me was that the Armenians were not loyal to the Ottoman Empire. The Turks believed that the Armenians favored the Russians in the war rather than the Turks.

WEIZMANN: They killed an entire people because they were worried about the loyalty of a few?

MORGENTHAU: They tried to. The governing class considered the Armenians to be disloyal. Remember, we are in a war, Dr. Weizmann; civilian loyalty is critical to the state. Let me come back to my earlier question. What could happen to the Jews in Germany if there is a perception of disloyalty in this war?

WEIZMANN: There won't be a perception of disloyalty.

MORGENTHAU: Can you predict with certainty the opinions of future German politicians? You are going to announce that the British favor a homeland for the Jews; but you doubt Germans are smart enough to deduce a connection.

WEIZMANN: If we don't win the war, the Germans will set the terms of the peace. If we win, we will set the terms. We will have a Jewish home in Palestine.

MORGENTHAU: So, we are two Zionists who have different visions. You would gain land by force, by moving the existing population off from the land as an act of war. I would gain land by buying it from the government which has ruled it for 400 years. You would put the future of Jews in other countries at risk by establishing a country where Jews exert unequal rights. I favor investing in a nation which honors the equal rights for all citizens.

WEIZMANN: Your proposal is impossible, sir.

MORGENTHAU: Why is that?

WEIZMANN: We have moved beyond it, now. At this point, the Americans are in the war.

MORGENTHAU: You are right about that, but if I can get the Turks to state reasonable terms, I might be able to stop this war before any Americans have even entered Europe. President Wilson is a man who professes peace.

WEIZMANN: You are not able to stop this war. You are only positioned to ruin the chance of Jews returning to Palestine after almost 1800 years.

MORGENTHAU: We differ only on methods, sir. We both want Jews to have the chance to return to Palestine. You believe that you can safely move into a neighborhood by seizing someone's property. I believe that long term peace with the neighbors will be better if you pay for any property you occupy.

WEIZMANN: You are going to stop this war and eliminate the chance for a Jewish homeland.

MORGENTHAU: You are going to prolong the war by nefarious means and put Jews who don't know and don't agree with your plan at risk.

WEIZMANN: Whatever our differences of approach, I think you must agree that what has been started cannot be stopped-- not now.

MORGENTHAU: I'm sorry to admit it, but yes, what you have started will be very difficult to stop without great loss of reputation of the Jewish people. Is it true that a Supreme Court justice is directing this secret operation while the American Secretary of State knows nothing about it?

WEIZMANN: You are not a journalist! It is important for you to confirm to me that you will not expose our efforts.

MORGENTHAU: I am a Jew, but I am also an American. What you have done offends me as a Jew as it does not consider my best instincts or interests; but it also offends me as an American. Americans will be deeply disturbed to know that they were manipulated into a war for a Jewish homeland. You have put my place in America at risk. How many Zionists are in on this? Ten? Fifteen? Only one Jew in a million even knows about this.

WEIZMANN: You do not speak for the Jewish nation, Mr. Ambassador.

MORGENTHAU: Neither do you, sir, but you and your small band of co-conspirators started your plan first and you will compromise the safety of millions. I can see now where this started but I can't see where it will end.

WEIZMANN: It will end with a great new nation of Jews!

Scene 8

Chaim Weizmann sits with a committee of his closest associates including Harry Sacher, LEON SIMON, Sokolow, SIEFF, MARKS, and Moses Gaster at London's Imperial Hotel on August 3, 1917.

WEIZMANN: I told him in no uncertain terms that organized Zionism will not enter into any kind of arrangement with the Turks which might be construed as a separate peace.

SIMON: Why? Why tie Zionism to the British war effort? It makes no sense. If the British are defeated, Zionism will never achieve its goal.

WEIZMANN: The British won't be defeated and therefore Zionism won't be defeated.

SIMON: The war is going to end. The Germans are looking for a peaceful solution, as are the British; and the Americans don't really want to even field an army in Europe.

WEIZMANN: The war is going to end but it will end with a British victory. Anything less is a failure for the Empire and therefore a failure for Zionism.

SIMON: I just wonder if we are not becoming too enamored of the secret schemes of Sir Mark Sykes. What will happen if news gets out that a Zionist was in Gibraltar trying to prevent a peace mission? Won't we be accused of prolonging the war?

WEIZMANN: It is the British who said the war was about the small nations. And Armenia, Syria, and Palestine are small nations-- repressed too long. Conquering Palestine for the British Empire is another buffer to protect the Suez Canal.

SACHER: Have you forgotten that Field Marshal Kitchener said that Palestine was of no military consequence for the Empire?

WEIZMANN: That was his opinion.

SACHER: Right, but all English people would accept his opinion over ours. We have obvious conflicts of interest.

WEIZMANN: You two young men are too pessimistic. The Allies will win this war and we will get our just rewards.

SACHER: "I see peril that we Zionists in England may be infected with imperialism at the very time when the rest of the world is beginning to cast it off." But more importantly, if we are seen to be prolonging the war in the interests of the Jews, we can expect a terrible backlash if the news were to become public. "I myself would not buy a British protectorate at the cost of prolonging the war by a single day."

WEIZMANN (after some contemplation): We have a choice to make. We have come a great distance in the last year. A dream which has lingered in the Jewish consciousness for 1800 years is within our grasp. Now I hear different voices rise, different objections being raised. We are waiting for the War Council to approve the declaration we wrote for them. Some of you look for reasons not to proceed. Some have objections which have some basis in truth and experience. If we wish to achieve this great goal, this is the moment to push it through.

SOKOLOW: Why might the War Council be delaying their endorsement of the declaration?

WEIZMANN: We know that various English Jews oppose our efforts.   Some of these Jews are very powerful;   some have very good arguments against the declaration; some have arguments against the establishment of a Jewish homeland.

SOKOLOW: The French--

WEIZMANN: --the French Jews are as divided as we are. This opportunity has not surfaced before in almost two thousand years of Jewish history and it is unlikely to ever happen again. Last spring, we raised the possibility with the government that the Germans were sending out feelers for an agreement with the international Jewish community.

SOKOLOW: It was a plausible idea: Herzl was an Austrian. The Germans might wish to guarantee a Jewish homeland in Palestine in exchange for the advantages that an alliance with international Jewry might provide.

WEIZMANN: We asked some of our friends in the German press to put out stories in Germany which reported that the government there is evaluating an alliance with the international Jews. They helped us, but still the British War Council delays. The problem is now that the Americans are mobilizing to enter the war, any leverage we have on the British will soon be exhausted. If we don't get their public endorsement soon, we may not get it at all.

SACHER: Zionism should not be linked to who wins the war. Zionism is independent of politics.

WEIZMANN: In an ideal world it would be independent of politics but in this world, it is very dependent. And we must push through whatever barriers we must to force the British to honor their agreement.

Scene 9

Louis Brandeis arrives at the desk of a White House secretary on September 12, 1917.

SECRETARY: Good afternoon, Justice Brandeis. The President is tied up. Would you like to speak to Colonel House?

BRANDEIS: I don't speak to Colonel House. I speak to the President. What's going on here?

SECRETARY: The President is in a meeting. He has only so much time in his day.

BRANDEIS: Who do you think you're talking to? You think I have extra time in my day?

SECRETARY: No, no. I know the President is always anxious to speak to you.

Colonel House opens his office door and looks out.

COLONEL HOUSE: Justice Brandeis, my goodness, I'm sorry we didn't have you properly ushered in. Did the President know you were coming?

BRANDEIS: Since when does Louis Brandeis need an appointment to talk with Woodrow Wilson?

COLONEL HOUSE: Please come into my office, Justice Brandeis, while we tell the President you are here.

Brandeis and House go into an office next to the Oval Office.

BRANDEIS: What the hell is going on here? I got a cable from London that says that the President does not want to sign off on the declaration.

HOUSE: The President does not believe the timing is quite right.

BRANDEIS: That's what I was told. President Wilson cabled that the time was "not opportune."

HOUSE: Yes. I wrote the cable to the War Cabinet in response to their inquiry as to the President's thoughts on the declaration.

BRANDEIS: You wrote the cable?

HOUSE: Yes. I discussed it with the President and he felt that endorsing the declaration for a Jewish homeland before American troops have entered the war will make it appear that the two are somehow related. He does not want the declaration to be linked to American entry into the war.

BRANDEIS: Of course not, but our understanding has been that I write any communications about the Palestine declaration. Anything coming from the President's office about Palestine goes through me.

HOUSE: That's a very unusual understanding, sir.

BRANDEIS: I don't care how unusual you think it is. It's the way things work here. I write the cables about Palestine.

HOUSE: I hadn't been aware---

BRANDEIS: --You're aware now.

President Wilson opens the door to Colonel House's office and enters. House rises.

HOUSE: Justice Brandeis is here to discuss the Palestine declaration, Mr. President.

WILSON: Yes. I worry what Americans might think if we support what amounts to an extension of the British Empire.

BRANDEIS: You have already committed to the war.

WILSON: I would prefer that our approval of the declaration not be made public right now.

BRANDEIS: We agreed that you would endorse the declaration when you were asked to by the people in London.

WILSON: I agreed to make my best efforts, but I'm afraid that if I endorse the declaration at the time the men are being drafted, we will face criticism that there is some connection between the declaration and American entry into the war.

BRANDEIS: Have you changed your mind about the declaration?

WILSON: Certainly not. I favor a homeland for the Jews.

BRANDEIS. It is a question of timing.

WILSON: You still have my support.

BRANDEIS: What if you cabled London that you give the declaration your endorsement, but you do not wish to make your endorsement public at this time. Would that be a reasonable compromise?

WILSON: Yes. I think so. Once the war has started and the public rallies to the cause, it will be unpatriotic to make negative comments about the war.

BRANDEIS: The Espionage Act has already passed and there is wide support for the addition of a Sedition Act to further prevent criticism of our war effort.

WILSON: We can't have malcontents waging criticisms while men are going into battle.

BRANDEIS: Why don't you ask Colonel House to write a cable to our friends in London to give them your support of the declaration but simply say that you will choose the appropriate time for your public endorsement. That way it will be less obvious that we are involved in the decision.

WILSON: I agree. Colonel House will prepare the cable.

BRANDEIS: Why waste time? I'll write the cable. I'll write it and you will approve it.

WILSON: Yes, you write it and I'll approve it. I'd like to read it before it is sent.

Scene 10

Chaim Weizmann and James Malcolm pace outside a meeting room at the Foreign Office on October 31, 1917. A meeting of the War Cabinet is in progress.

WEIZMANN: Wouldn't you know that it would be a Jew who would try to block the declaration!

MALCOLM: Could have been anyone. Could have been an anti-Semite.

WEIZMANN: Montagu says that the anti-Semites all favor the declaration believing it will get the Jews out of England.

MALCOLM: It's too bad we don't have a supportive Jew in the cabinet right now.

WEIZMANN: Did you read Montagu's memorandum?

MALCOLM: Lord Montagu can be very persuasive.

WEIZMANN: He asserts that there is no Jewish nation. He denies that Palestine is today associated with Jews or that it is a proper place for Jews to live. He claims that if we name Palestine as the home for the Jewish people, the outcome will be that we "vitally prejudice the position of every Jew elsewhere." How can he serve the government in India if the British government comes out with a statement that it believes "his home is not in England but in Palestine"?

MALCOLM: The good news is that by being named India Secretary, he is now out of the country. So, the War Cabinet is in there debating his memorandum but he himself is on his way to India.

WEIZMANN: Thank God.

MALCOLM: We finally got President Wilson's blessing.

WEIZMANN: None of this would have been possible without Justice Brandeis. He's the one who told Wilson that if the Allies don't move on the declaration, the Germans might become interested in an alliance with World Jewry.

MALCOLM: Is that true?

WEIZMANN: Who knows about the truth? It was reported in the German press, but it was news to the German government.

They laugh.

MALCOLM: Poor Lord Montagu: he's an English Jew, through and through, and yet he believes he is a Jewish Englishman. I wonder if the distinction is really so important. Surely there is room in this world for English Jews who wish to live in England and English Jews who wish to live in Palestine.

WEIZMANN: Of course there is and there will be room in Palestine for Jews from America and from Germany and from Russia-- especially for Jews from Russia. As the world becomes a better place, Jews will have citizenship in the countries of their choice. We plan to build a society in Palestine which is every bit as fair and just as the democracies of the west-- more just-- but finally, at long last, Jews will have a land of origin that we control!

(The door to the meeting room opens and Sir Mark Sykes leaves by himself.)

SYKES (from a distance): "It's a boy."

(Malcolm and Weizmann hug each other.)

WEIZMANN: "Mazel Tov! Mazel Tov!"

(Weizmann and Malcolm jump in their excitement while Sir Mark walks in the opposite direction. Coming to the opposite side of the stage, he stops, turns, and walks back toward Chaim Weizmann. The two shake hands as the lights dim.)

Scene 11

Woodrow Wilson sits at his desk in the Oval Office in 1918. When Horace Kallen enters his office, Wilson rises from his desk with his chin tilted slightly up.

WILSON: How long has it been since you first entered my office at Princeton, Horace?

KALLEN: Funny, I was just trying to come up with that number while I was waiting outside.

WILSON: You've come a long way from that first job as an English instructor, haven't you?

KALLEN: It has been close to 15 years since our first meeting at Princeton and, yes, I've come a long way. I suppose anyone might say that you also have traveled quite a distance.

WILSON: We are only servants of God, Horace. We go where He directs us.

KALLEN: You remain strong in your faith.

WILSON: Justice Brandeis always told me that you were the one who convinced him to become a Zionist.

KALLEN: I just convinced him that Jews can be proud of their identity: it is possible to be a good Jew and be a good American.

WILSON: To be a good Jew, you must be a good Zionist.

KALLEN: That's what Justice Brandeis said but I have my doubts.

WILSON: You have doubts?

KALLEN: I think good Jews can support Zionism and good Jews can want to live without religion.

WILSON: A Jew living a secular life?

KALLEN: My father's a rabbi and I live a secular life. Everyone finds his own way.

WILSON: I understand that you have gotten in trouble up in Wisconsin.

KALLEN: I suppose so.

WILSON: You want me to give you a presidential pardon.

KALLEN: No, not for me.

WILSON: I heard that you lost your job.

KALLEN: Yes, sir, I did; but I lost my job at the university for defending the right of a young man to oppose the war. It is a pardon for him that I seek.

WILSON: You would defend the right of someone to criticize our war efforts?

KALLEN: The right to criticize is at the core of our beliefs, Mr. President. If we don't have the right to criticize and discuss our political actions, we have nothing worth defending.

WILSON: Young men from farms and small towns all across this country have been drafted into the army and are now being torn to pieces in France for a war that you favored.

KALLEN: It is not that I don't support the war.

WILSON: You were as important as Justice Brandeis in pushing for American entry into the war.

KALLEN: I support the soldiers in the field. It's just that I must support the right of an individual to disagree with anything in this society. It's what makes it a free society.

WILSON: We will have no criticism of the war while I am sending young men to die in the trenches of France.

KALLEN: The Sedition Act makes it illegal for anyone to say anything critical of the war.

WILSON: I signed that act and the Supreme Court upheld that act.

KALLEN: I understand, sir. I was not critical of the war. I was critical of the law that forbids open debate. We are a democracy and a democracy only works if we have a free press and we are free to voice our disagreements.

WILSON: Not on my watch, young man. The war is on; men are dying in the fields of France; and we will not debate whether they are dying for some back-room agreement about which they know nothing.

KALLEN: I remember people always said that Woodrow Wilson listened to all positions before he made decisions.

WILSON: I think that is true.

KALLEN: After you listened to different ideas, you made a judgement as to what was right.

WILSON: That is what my father taught me to do. He was a minister.

KALLEN: You stood firm by your principles even when criticism was waged.

WILSON: That is my character.

KALLEN: Yes, sir. I understand.

WILSON (voice rising): We shall overcome the German defenses and we shall conquer them, and then we shall require that they pay for the conflict which they unleashed on this world. We will impose a peace treaty on them which the world will never forget.

KALLEN: Yes. I can see that now.

WILSON: (more composed) What will you do without a job, Horace?

KALLEN: I'm meeting with some friends in New York City. We're thinking of founding a new school there?

WILSON: A new school?

KALLEN: Yes. A place where anyone can make an argument for anything. In the process of having discussions and debates, we hope that we will generate perspective on decisions, and hopefully wisdom from the process.

WILSON: I wish you well, Horace. I cannot agree with your defense of a worthless protester, but I wish you well.

KALLEN: I appreciate your good wishes, Mr. President. From the light of your example, I now can see the error of my ways.

Two of J. A. Jensen's great uncles fought with the Allies in France during World War I.

Interview with the author:

Q: Why have we never heard of the Sykes-Weizmann agreement?

A: The most obvious answer is that it represented a secret operation. No serious historian doubts that there was an agreement made between Sir Mark Sykes and Dr. Chaim Weizmann on February 7, 1917. There may be some discussion as to what exactly was agreed upon, but no one doubts that there was an agreement and that Weizmann was given access to British Foreign Office communication facilities to communicate the news.

Q: How is it possible that such a story could have remained unreported?

A: In fact, it was reported. Samuel Landman, the Zionist lawyer, first detailed the agreement in 1936 and he referred to Professor Harold Temperley's comprehensive history of the Paris peace accord from 1920. Former Prime Minister David Lloyd George testified a few months after Landman that the Zionists had been very important in bringing America into the war and he questioned whether the British would keep their commitment to the Zionists. James Malcolm wrote his first-person account of the agreement in 1944 while German planes were bombing London. If the agreement had been known publicly at the time, America would have never entered World War I. It is easy to see why the agreement was a secret then and why few people want to discuss it now.

Q: Anti-Semites have traditionally blamed the Jews for almost every bad thing in history. Why isn't this just another example of trying to blame the Jews for something that no one understands?

A. This play doesn't blame "the Jews" for anything. It dramatizes how a small group of Zionists, including an Armenian Christian, a Supreme Court justice, and a British aristocrat, among others, secretly conspired to bring the United States into World War I. The war was at a stalemate. Without American intervention, it is likely that a peace would have been negotiated in early 1917. Instead, Chaim Weizmann and Mark Sykes agreed on the deal proposed by Horace Kallen: if the British would endorse Zionist aspirations in Palestine, powerful forces of American Zionists would encourage the entry of the United States into the war. The play illustrates how Jewish opinion was divided at the time on the goals and methods of Zionism and it also illustrates that very few Jews and very few Englishmen had any idea that the agreement was being made.

Q: Why did the British seek the approval of President Wilson for the wording of the Balfour Declaration?

A: Obviously, the American president was involved in the negotiation on some level. That the British cabinet insisted on President Wilson's approval of the final wording of the declaration proves American involvement. After he met with President Wilson in May 1917, British foreign minister Arthur Balfour met with Justice Louis Brandeis for breakfast at a Washington hotel. Balfour didn't meet privately with any other justices of the Supreme Court, any representatives of the Department of State, or any members of Congress. I don't think it was simply a coincidence that the director of the Parushim met with Balfour.

Q: How can you be certain that there was a Parushim?

A: The existence of the Parushim was researched and published by the Israeli historian Sarah Schmidt. In the 1970's, after interviewing Horace Kallen, Schmidt disclosed letters and other documentation of the society (which are preserved in the American Jewish Archives in Cincinnati). Keep in mind that it was a secret society-- allegiance was demanded and oaths were sworn to secrecy. Schmidt was a historian and took her role very seriously. To her great credit, she did not try to hide the involvement of Louis Brandeis. Other historians, including former *New York Times* reporter and editor Peter Grose in his book <u>Israel in the Mind of America</u>, document this secret organization.

Q: You show Justice Brandeis encouraging President Wilson to change his mind about approving the Balfour Declaration. How can you be sure it was Brandeis?

A: That's a great question because this is a play of historical fiction. No one knows for sure what was said at various meetings unless there are written records-- as in some cases there are, and, in those cases, I put quotation marks around whatever was recorded. In the example you cite, the historian Bruce Allen Murphy asserts in his award-winning book <u>The Brandeis-Frankfurter Connection</u> that the diaries of Colonel House prove that it was Brandeis who was able to get President Wilson to reverse his "not opportune" stance on the Balfour Declaration.

Q: Do you have similar documentation for the discussion between Ambassador Morgenthau and Chaim Weizmann?

A: No, I'm not aware of any original records of their meeting at Gibraltar on July 5, 1917. Chaim Weizmann recounted his memory of everyone speaking in German at the Gibraltar meeting in his autobiography <u>Trial and Error</u>. I am unaware of an official transcript of that historic discussion. Weizmann also wrote that Senator Reed blamed him (in 1922) for "prolonging the war for two years." A veteran of the war, Reed was one of the co-sponsors of the Immigration Act of 1924 which sharply limited Jewish and southern European immigration into the United States. If Weizmann's scuttling of the Morgenthau mission was known to Pennsylvania Senator David Reed, can we imagine it was unknown to the newly organized Nazis? Samuel Landman's statement in 1936 that the agreement was known to the Germans and the basis for much of the "Nazi programme" of anti-Semitism reflected the reality that the secret gentlemen's agreement was not as secret as its makers had hoped.

Q: Why didn't you write this play as a non-fiction work? Your readers are going to want to know how much of it really happened.

A: Much of this history has been written as non-fiction. It is surprising that so few people have heard about the Sykes-Weizmann agreement, but that reality only underscores that the agreement has been regarded as too sensitive to even assign a name and the silence has been maintained well into the 21st century. One hundred years have now passed since the agreement was made and it is appropriate for us to evaluate its outcomes.

Q: Do you believe that conflict in the Middle East is related to the Sykes-Weizmann agreement?

A: I can't imagine anyone coming to any other conclusion. It is hard to understand the agreement for what it was and not believe that it had a great impact on everything that followed in the 20th century. If we don't have the courage to even consider this chapter of history, we can't knowledgeably address the conflict in the Middle East.

Q: The Sykes-Weizmann agreement was made in February 1917. That was before the Russian Revolution. Do you believe that the agreement somehow influenced the course of history in Russia?

A: I think questions like that are impossible to know. I am aware of Winston Churchill's alleged comment to the publisher of the *New York Enquirer* in 1936. It's an amazing summation which sounds like something the historian Churchill said but something the politician Churchill tried to disavow a few years later when he was trying to convince the United States to enter World War II. Churchill was quoted as saying: "America should have minded her own business and stayed out of the World War. If you hadn't entered the war, the Allies would have made peace with Germany in the Spring of 1917. Had we made peace then there would have been no collapse in Russia followed by Communism, no breakdown in Italy followed by Fascism, and Germany would not have signed the Versailles Treaty, which has enthroned Nazism in Germany."

Q: Samuel Landman wrote his account of the Sykes-Weizmann agreement in 1936; then, a few months later, David Lloyd George testified to the House of Commons about why he approved the agreement; and later that year, Winston Churchill criticized American entry into a war he believed should have stopped in the Spring of 1917. What was going on that brought out all these opinions in 1936?

A: No one knows for sure, but the Nazi disaster was unfolding in Germany.

Q: You say "Nazi disaster" but your play sounds like you have sympathy for the Germans. Which is it?

A: Let me be completely clear: I have great sympathy for the Germans and no sympathy for the Nazis. Ethnic nationalism will not promote peace and genocide must always be condemned.

Q: Do you believe that the agreement remains a secret?

A: Certain facts are accepted. Comprehensive histories have detailed the meetings between the English Zionists and Sir Mark Sykes. For reasons that are not clear to me, these historians do not mention that Justice Brandeis directed a secret society devoted to a new Jewish commonwealth in Palestine. Neither is Samuel Landman's explanation of the Sykes-Weizmann agreement widely quoted, nor the historical narrative written by James Malcolm. Both men were eye-witnesses. Louis Brandeis's involvement in American endorsement of the Balfour Declaration is undisputed, but some historians fail to mention Horace Kallen's secret society or Brandeis's direction of its members.

Q: Might those historians be conflicted about reporting on something which might embarrass Zionism?

A: Well, it is easy to see how some historians might feel conflicted; but Sarah Schmidt, the Israeli historian who first wrote about the Parushim, put her duties as a historian above her desire to avoid embarrassment for Zionism.

Q: Do you believe that discussion of the Sykes-Weizmann agreement might provoke anti-Semitism in the modern world?

A: Surely you must mean more anti-Semitism. Readers should see that this agreement was the work of only a small number of British war ministers and a small number of Zionists. Only one Jew in a million even knew about the agreement. On one level, the agreement led to the establishment of the modern State of Israel. Most people would say that is not an anti-Semtic outcome. However, on another level, if this agreement motivated anti-Semitism in post-World War I Germany, as asserted by Zionist lawyer Samuel Landman, and if it motivated the Johnson-Reed Immigration Act of 1924 in the United States, then it is arguably the single most anti-Semitic action in all of history.

Q: Does the Sykes-Weizmann Agreement make you question American support for Israel?

A: No, it only shows that the United States was involved from the beginning. It demonstrates why the United States, England, and France all bear some responsibility to support a just peace in the Middle East. As Israel currently occupies the West Bank and restricts and confines Palestinians, I don't believe we have a lasting peace in the region yet. To me, that means we should do more peacemaking in the area and less war making; more scholarship programs to the United States and fewer walls and tanks.

Q: Do you think the Sykes-Weizmann Agreement was a legally binding contract?

A: It's hard for me to see it as a legally binding contract. Samuel Landman, the Zionist lawyer in London in 1917, saw it as a *quid pro quo* contract but under what jurisdiction would such a contract be judged? I'm unaware of a written copy of the agreement. British copyright laws might still be more powerful than the public's right to know, as they were when Professor Harold Temperley wrote about the Treaty of Versailles in 1920.

Q: Does knowledge of this agreement bring into question the legitimacy of Israel?

A: No, Israel is now a sovereign state and it isn't going to suddenly disappear. Justice will not be achieved in the Middle East by threatening the security of Israel. The play is only intended to help people understand the historical context of the times. From the Pittsburg program, we know that Horace Kallen and Louis Brandeis favored a state where Palestinians could hold land and would have civil rights. I believe that we will make better decisions about how to proceed with Middle East policy if we have a balanced historical account of how the world arrived at this juncture.

It is interesting to wonder how Jewish colonization might have proceeded in the absence of the Sykes-Weizmann agreement. Jewish philanthropists had purchased areas of Palestine prior to World War I. Had Henry Morgenthau's mission to Turkey not been scuttled by Chaim Weizmann and Felix Frankfurter at Gibraltar in July 1917, it is quite possible that Morgenthau would have negotiated a separate peace with Turkey, ended the war, and succeeded in purchasing large tracts of Palestine. We should realize that Jewish re-colonization of the area did not necessarily require prolongation of the war. Negotiation always trumps savagery.

Q: Does your story suggest that open democratic governments should avoid secret agreements?

A: Yes, I think so. It is ironic that Woodrow Wilson articulated the goal that our ostensibly transparent and democratic government seek only "open covenants for peace, openly arrived at." This is a story of how men with the best of intentions, men with high motives, made a secret agreement which might have had unspeakable consequences. And it demonstrates how the fate of millions can be secretly influenced by a small number of conflicted parties at the center of democratically elected governments.

Q: How can you say that men who plotted to extend World War I had the best of intentions?

A: I can't really. It's hard for me to overlook the deaths caused by extension of the war, but I believe Sykes and Weizmann believed the agreement was good for the people they represented. I agree with President Wilson before he changed his stripes: someone should have represented "friends of humanity in every nation" and insisted on a "peace without victory." War kills too many innocent people to be used as a tool for any kind of change.

Q: Are you suggesting that we shouldn't be at war in the Middle East today?

A: The play is only about what happened prior to 1919, so I can't say the play addresses questions about the modern day. The play demonstrates the horrors of resolving ethnic rivalries or border disputes using violence. What did society learn from the 20th century? Did the impulse to use force work well or might peaceful approaches have been better? What worked better in post-World War II Europe: were we right to have a policy of containment rather than a policy of annihilation? War destroys; peace creates. It is as simple as that. However, peace must be maintained by a strong military presence-- ideally shared by the international community of nations. Ultimately, we would all agree that the greatest defender of peace is justice.

Q: You suggest in the play that President Wilson was compromised by a secret relationship and that Louis Brandeis helped him manage what might have been a public relations disaster during an election year. Did you make that up?

A: No, I'm afraid not. Woodrow Wilson developed an extramarital relationship with a woman while he was still at Princeton and the relationship continued while he was governor and president. The most embarrassing letters were no doubt destroyed but some survive. Certain "humanitarian" payments were made to Mary Allen Hulbert and at least one source wrote that Louis Brandeis was rumored (in 1916) to be Wilson's agent in the matter. If the secret records of the Parushim are ever made freely available to scholars or the public, historians might further examine this part of the mystery. Similarly, we don't know if or to what extent Zionists were involved in anti-German publicity in 1917. The release of the complete secret files of the Parushim might provide more information. We must hope the records of the Parushim will not suffer the same fate as some of Mary Allen Hulbert's letters.

Q: How can you say that your play is not anti-Semitic if it causes embarassment for Zionism?

A: A dramatization of history, of the agreement which may have prompted American entry into World War I, is not by itself anti-Semitic. This play does not condemn or demean the Jewish people. Quite the opposite: this play illustrates that very few Jews were aware of the agreement and that Jews possessed a wide diversity of opinion about Zionism at the time. Jews were disproportionately injured by the outcome of the agreement. I'm sure that many Zionists who know this story wish, as I do, that Robert Morgenthau had succeeded in his mission to buy land in Palestine and cancelled the arrival of American soldiers in Europe. Is it anti-Semitic to know certain history? Or, it is anti-Semitic to perpetuate the long standing secret and hope that ignorance can enlighten policy in the Middle East? While we should be careful about discussing history which might offend some readers, let me argue that people who had no idea that there was ever an agreement made in February 1917 lost their lives, or their sons' lives, or their husbands' lives in World War I. Many, many more people died in World War II. Shouldn't all history be discussed regardless of who it offends? I'm against anti-Semitism, that's for sure, but I'm also against selective and sanitized history. Think of my views as being against war rather than being against one ethnic or religious group. War has been very hard on people of all ethnicities.

Q: Do you believe that the onerous conditions of the Treaty of Versailles forced the world into another war?

A: Churchill would have agreed with that statement in 1936, but it is beyond the subject matter of this play. This play examines the question of whether Zionism played a role in the entry of the United States into World War I. It cannot determine with certainty the motivation of President Wilson or members of the House of Representatives, or what the most important factors were in their final decision to declare war, but asking such questions is an important and well recognized function of historical fiction.

Made in the USA
Middletown, DE
07 March 2022